BUMBLEBEE™ at SUPER HERO HIGH

BUMBLEBEE™
at SUPER HERO HIGH

By Lisa Yee

Random House 🏠 New York

To Dennis S.,
a great editor and secret super hero

Copyright © 2018 DC Comics.
DC SUPER HERO GIRLS and all related characters and elements
© & TM DC Comics and Warner Bros. Entertainment Inc.
WB SHIELD: TM & © WBEI. (s18)
RHUS39931

All rights reserved. Published in the United States by Random House Children's
Books, a division of Penguin Random House LLC, New York, and in Canada by
Penguin Random House Canada Limited, Toronto. Random House and the colophon
are registered trademarks of Penguin Random House LLC.
Visit us on the Web!
rhcbooks.com
dcsuperherogirls.com
dckids.com
Library of Congress Cataloging-in-Publication Data
Name: Yee, Lisa, author.
Title: Bumblebee at Super Hero High / by Lisa Yee.
Description: New York : Random House, [2018] | Series: DC Super Hero girls
Identifiers: LCCN 2018001882 | ISBN 978-1-5247-6926-0 (hardback) |
ISBN 978-1-5247-6927-7 (lib. bdg.) | ISBN 978-1-5247-6928-4 (ebook)
Subjects: | BISAC: JUVENILE FICTION / Comics & Graphic Novels /
Media Tie-In. | JUVENILE FICTION / Comics & Graphic Novels / Superheroes. |
JUVENILE FICTION / Action & Adventure / General.
Classification: LCC PZ7.Y3638 Bu 2018 | DDC [Fic]—dc23

Printed in the United States of America
10 9 8 7 6 5 4 3 2 1

PROLOGUE

The green kangaroo refused to stop hopping. Instead, he kept photobombing Harley Quinn while she was videoing herself being videoed by a teen reporter from Metropolis High, as bystanders videoed both of them with their phones.

"You've been named Super Hero High's Super Hero of the Month," said Lois Lane. "During a crucial battle, you even turned off your cameras, which meant your popular web show, *Harley's Quinntessentials,* was off the air. Then, while your web empire went dark, you captured the evil Mad Hatter without anyone watching! What's next for Harley Quinn?"

Harley, who had suddenly done a handstand, was upside down when she replied, "What's next is whatever's new!"

"Over here!" the green kangaroo called out while waving from the sidelines. "Look at me!"

"Stop that," Bumblebee whispered. Beast Boy could be so annoying sometimes. "*Shhhh!*"

While most of her friends were inside Capes & Cowls Café enjoying the towering "Congrats, Harley!" cake that shot sprinkles from the top, Bumblebee was outside watching the interview with interest. Harley looked totally confident. Super Hero High's class clown was a natural super hero who basked in the attention, unlike Bumblebee, who wasn't nearly as comfortable with the spotlight that sometimes came with saving the world.

Beast Boy would not stop hopping. "Calm down," Bumblebee told him again. "This is about Harley, not you."

"Aw, you're no fun," Beast Boy grumbled as he morphed back into a furry green teen with pointy ears and purple high-tops. Not able to keep a sour face for long, he poked Bumblebee and said, "Hey, buzzzzzz, wanna play freeze tag?"

Before Bumblebee could say "No, thank you," Frost sauntered past and used her powers to freeze Beast Boy in place. Just then, Bumblebee's phone rang. The familiar "Flight of the Bumblebee" ringtone signaled her mother calling.

"Hey, Mom, what's up?" Bumblebee stepped away so as not to disturb Harley's interview. "What's that? I'm having trouble hearing you. I thought you said 'bad news.'"

"I did," Ms. Andrena-Beecher said. Her normally warm and comforting voice trembled. "Oh, honey, first I want you to know that your father and I are safe. His arm is broken, but we're fine. The damage, though, was pretty bad—"

"The damage? What damage?" Bumblebee's heart began to race. "Mom, what happened?"

"The tree . . . the crash . . . house destroyed . . . ," her mother tried to explain.

Bumblebee began to gasp for air. Supergirl, who had wandered out of the café carrying a plate of cake, rushed over. "Are you okay?" she asked.

Harley glanced at the commotion and cut off her interview with Lois Lane. "Bumblebee?" she said, bounding over to her friend. "**WHOA** and **WOWZA!** You look like you've seen a ghost."

By then Bumblebee was picturing the worst. She always got high marks in creative writing at school—but now her imagination was in overdrive.

Beast Boy, who was standing closest to Bumblebee, threw his hands up in the air defensively. "Not my fault!" he insisted. "I think she just got some bad news." He reached out and relieved Supergirl of the cake she was still holding.

Bumblebee nodded. Before Beast Boy could take a bite of cake, she flew away, leaving her friends worrying and wondering what had just happened.

PART ONE

CHAPTER 1

Most bees can fly fifteen to twenty miles per hour, max. But Karen "Bumblebee" Andrena-Beecher wasn't most bees. Her last name came from her mother, Andria Andrena, and her father, Rob Beecher, but Karen's nickname was all her own.

Karen had always loved technology and science, almost as much as she loved pretending to be a super hero. On her fifth birthday, Mr. and Ms. Andrena-Beecher had given their daughter her first engineering kit. In no time, she created a set of girl-sized bee wings that oscillated, rather than rotated, to create an aerodynamic force for maximum airspeed. Needless to say, her parents were more than a little surprised to find their five-year-old daughter hovering in the air on homemade bee wings. After they finished applauding, Mr. Andrena-Beecher reached for his camera and Ms. Andrena-Beecher said, "Honey, don't get too close to the ceiling fan."

"Look at me!" Karen cried out gleefully. "I'm just like the super heroes!"

As Karen grew older, she moved from plastic gears to metal ones, from flashlight batteries to mega electrical chargers. She studied robotics and chemistry and engineering. Sure, she occasionally blew things up in the Bee Tree Lab, as she had dubbed her tree house. But explosions—or "slight miscalculations," as she liked to call them—were all part of the "learning process," Karen would tell her parents. And she was plenty safe in her lab. She had designed it herself and then built it with her mother, an architect famous for her ecofriendly tiny houses.

Her father, a photographer, would ride the hydraulic lift Karen had constructed to get to the lab, which towered two stories above their house. He would bring his daughter cameras to fix, ask for help updating the software on his computer, and solicit advice on jump-starting the electric car she had saved from the junkyard and given him on Father's Day.

It was in the Bee Tree Lab that Karen first bonded with the friendly bees who had set up a hive on one of the top branches. Their constant buzz was sweet music to her ears. Karen loved nothing more than to listen to them as she snacked on crisp apple slices dipped in sweet golden honey while she experimented with her tech. One slow day, while talking to the bees, one accidentally stung her. Instead of getting upset, Karen merely removed the stinger to study it.

The tiny stinger had a huge effect. It was as if the sting had jolted her brain into high gear. Immediately, she harkened back to when she had first created her bee wings. Bees. They weren't the question. They were the answer! Later that week, Karen developed a technology that would change the course of her life forever.

As Bumblebee soared past the tall buildings of downtown Metropolis, several office workers looked out their skyscraper windows and waved. Thanks to *Harley's Quinntessentials*, everyone knew who Bumblebee and her high school super-hero friends were. How could they not? Harley's web channel was a worldwide phenomenon, and her hidden cameras, which often caught Super Hero High students messing up, were huge hits. But there *were* also the Save the Day segments, in which Harley documented her friends risking their lives in lifesaving rescues. Because of this, many Supers had their own fan clubs, like the Wonders, devoted to all things Wonder Woman, and the FashioniStars, who followed everything Star Sapphire did and wore. Plus there were BTWs, aka Batgirl Tech Wizards. And then there were the Honey Bees, a group of fans who adored Bumblebee.

The office workers were waving and jumping up and down at the sight of Bumblebee soaring past. She tried to smile, but it was almost impossible when worry was propelling her. Thanks to her super-secret self-made technology, Bumblebee was able to fly and project powerful sonic blasts. Her enhanced strength was often underestimated, given her cheery demeanor, sparkly big brown eyes, and ever-present smile. But Bumblebee's best weapon was her ability to shrink on command. Few noticed her when she was the size of an insect, and unlike Giganta, the villain who towered over buildings and was never known to make a stealth entrance, a bee-sized Bumblebee could catch evildoers off guard.

Bumblebee pressed a button on her yellow super-suit top and shrank down. Her ultralight black leggings and yellow boots gave her an aerodynamic boost. All that was on Bumblebee's mind was that she needed to get home as soon as possible.

CHAPTER 2

Bumblebee soared over neighborhood landmarks, like Shealy's Corner Market, where she bought Gooey Honey Crunch candy. She looked down at the park where, when she was a toddler, she used to lie on her stomach across the swings, feet and arms extended as if she were flying. But as Bumblebee approached her street, she slowed.

In shock, she flew circles around her house—or at least, where her house had once stood. Below, in a smoldering heap, was what was left of the yellow two-story structure with white-shuttered windows. Off to the side, holding hands, were Mr. and Ms. Andrena-Beecher, talking to EMTs and police.

Bumblebee took a deep breath before landing and turning human-sized. "Mom? Dad?" She gathered them in a loving—and rather strong—embrace.

"Whoa! Ouch. Watch the arm," her father said, attempting to sound jolly.

Bumblebee stepped back and noticed his left arm tucked into a sling. "What happened?" she asked.

"It was a freak accident," Ms. Andrena-Beecher struggled to explain. "The police think termites got to the tree and then the tree fell . . ."

". . . on the house," Mr. Andrena-Beecher continued. "And it cut through some electrical wires, setting it on fire and causing some of your tech to explode."

"Karen—er, Bumblebee," her mom went on, "honey, there's not much left of the house or your lab."

Bumblebee nodded as she surveyed the damage. Most of the house was gone, except for a few things the firefighters had been able to rescue, like a gold-framed photo her father had taken of her when she'd first begun perfecting her flight suit. While some kids had school pictures on the walls to commemorate each year of school, Bumblebee's dad had taken an annual flight photo.

Ms. Andrena-Beecher hugged the photo tight. "We were lucky. This could have been much worse."

Bumblebee studied the remains of her tech lab. It was a mess. Then again, it was always a mess. But this was a mess times a hundred. A broken triple-action motor controller here, a shattered ultrasonic range finder there, and rubble everywhere. She felt a queasy sensation in her stomach when she saw the original battery pack she had worked on for her first super suit. Half of it was melted, like a honeycomb candy bar left in the sun. The latest and far more sophisticated version of the battery wasn't in much better shape. And her backup super suit was missing entirely—probably somewhere in the rubble.

Bumblebee recalled the day she'd finally gotten her super suit to work, years earlier. Her father had been frightened, and her mother had been wary when Karen began to shrink.

"She knows what she's doing," her mother said. Then she added, "Please tell me I'm right, Karen."

Thrilled, their daughter flew around the room, buzzing over the tops of their heads, before turning back to her regular size. "I did it!" she said, her eyes shining.

Her mother reached for her father's hand. "She did it," she said.

Mr. Andrena-Beecher nodded. "I guess I know what this means," he said solemnly.

Karen wanted to laugh and cry at the same time. "Yes, yes," she said. "I'm on my way to becoming a super hero! So now, when I'm old enough, can I apply to Super Hero High?"

Her dad shook his head no; her mom nodded yes. "We'll have to have some family meetings and discuss this, Karen," Ms. Andrena-Beecher said.

"But you promised," she reminded them. "Dad, you

said, 'Karen, if you can figure out how to shrink, you can do anything you want!'"

"Yes, but . . ." Her father stumbled over his words.

Karen hugged him. "I know," she said, smiling. "You didn't really think I could do it. But surprise!"

"Surprise indeed, Karen," her mother said, beaming with pride.

"*Bumblebee!*" their young daughter replied in a moment of inspiration. "Mom, Dad, from now on my name is Bumblebee."

CHAPTER 3

"**B**umblebee," Ms. Andrena-Beecher said, brushing the thick, wavy brown hair off her only child's face. There was a deep swatch of caramel color in it that looked like sunshine. "I'm so glad you weren't in the Bee Tree Lab when this happened. You might have gotten hurt."

Bumblebee tried not to laugh. Her parents were always worried about her. That was why she played down the danger of the battles she fought. "You know the news channels—they make things seem so much bigger than they really are," Bumblebee would say. This was the strategy lots of Super Hero High students used with their families.

"I'm sorry I wasn't around when the tree fell," Bumblebee said. "I could have stopped it. I should have been here."

It was rare for her to skip visiting her parents on Sunday; however, Bumblebee had planned to stay at school to work on an extra-credit project for Mr. Fox's Weaponomics class. She had a 97 percent average in the class, and the extra credit would have brought her up to 99. Also, there was Harley's Super Hero of the Month party.

"How?" Mr. Andrena-Beecher asked. "How could you have stopped it? It was nature taking its course."

"The termites must have been working away at this tree for months. Something this big just doesn't topple overnight," Ms. Andrena-Beecher observed.

Bumblebee nodded. Still, she felt funny inside. After all, wasn't she the super hero in the family? Wasn't it her job to thwart disasters? Her parents could have been seriously hurt, or worse. Surely there was something she could have done. As Mr. and Ms. Andrena-Beecher talked with the neighbors, who showed up bearing cookies and thermoses of coffee, Bumblebee returned to what was left of her lab.

She picked up her poster of Mary Jackson, a trailblazing African American engineer who worked for NASA, and smoothed it out. Tape could fix that tear in Mary's nose. Bumblebee rolled up the poster so that no more damage could be done. For the most part, her tech lab lay crushed and in pieces on the ground.

The police came over and began putting yellow and black caution tape around the scene, forcing her to back away. Besides, not much was left anyway. There were piles of wires and cables, melted metal and control panels. She saw some tech tools scattered about, but most were broken and could not be salvaged.

Bumblebee tried not to shed a tear. That would be silly, right? Everyone was safe. That was what truly mattered. Still, she had a hard time reconciling herself to the fact that her lab was gone—and that meant so were her projects.

"My parents are staying with my cousin Keisha's family while the house is rebuilt," Bumblebee explained. She was back in her room at school, surrounded by friends: Poison Ivy, Big Barda, and Batgirl. Wonder Woman and Supergirl dropped in to offer condolences. And Harley volunteered to do an exclusive video as a fundraising effort for the family.

"Thanks," Bumblebee said, holding up her hand to block Harley's video camera. "But this is nothing compared to true natural disasters happening all over the world."

"It's amazing no one got seriously hurt," said Batgirl as she took off her purple hoodie and shook out her auburn hair. "What will you do next?"

"Next . . . for what?" Bumblebee asked. She wondered how long it would take for her dad's broken arm to heal so he could start taking photos again.

"Your tech lab. All your stuff. Your experiments," Batgirl reminded her.

Bumblebee fell onto her bed and hugged her pillow. "Urgggggh!" she cried. "My lab!"

"Tea time!" announced Katana as she did a shoulder roll into the room, landed upright, and set down a tray.

"Thanks!" Bumblebee savored a sip of the warm ginger tea. She was glad Katana had added extra extra honey, just the way she liked it. "I guess I'll have to put everything on hold for a while. It's too bad; I was developing a new battery pack, one with a much longer life. I've been having problems with my current one. I think it's just too old. I'm lucky it's lasted this long."

CHAPTER 4

The teen super heroes sat still in the classroom as a dark storm descended upon them. What looked like sizzling bolts of fire ricocheted off the walls, bounced off the ceiling, and slammed into the floor, only to rebound and strike the oversized computer screens that flanked the back of the room. The thunder was so loud it created shock waves that caused the building to shake off its foundation.

Beast Boy tried to cover his ears with his hands, which was difficult because he had morphed into an elephant. Cheetah closed her eyes against the lightning. Miss Martian disappeared.

"Don't move, don't move," the teacher ordered. Bumblebee didn't even blink. "And ready . . . NOW!" shouted Mr. Fox.

With that command, the Supers sprang into action. The Flash ran around the Weaponomics room in an attempt to deflect the bolts Lightning kept throwing, while her sister, Thunder, amped up the loud crackling noises as her brown eyes twinkled with delight. Lightning adjusted the yellow headband that kept her short brown hair in place, and Thunder stomped her bright yellow boots, making the noise reverberate even more. It wasn't often that the sisters were asked to use the full force of their powers in the classroom. They were having a blast!

Star Sapphire flipped her long, dark hair over her shoulder, then aimed the lavender glow of her power ring at Thunder to distract her. Bumblebee used the sonic bee stings from her wrist-mounted blasters to diffuse the sound waves of the thunder. Wonder Woman used the Lasso of Truth to ground several lightning bolts at once, while Supergirl shot her heat vision at the sizzling bolt that was hurled at her. The force of the two forces smashing against each other caused an explosion that blew out the classroom windows.

Harley Quinn was thrilled. "**WOWZA** and **BAM!**" she shouted. She had gotten it all on camera. It was the perfect scene for her "Super School Strikes Again" segment on her web channel.

"Okay, stop, stop, just stop!" Mr. Fox said wearily. He had seen it all before. Today, the teacher was wearing his orange vest and gray sports jacket. "Everyone, take your seats. Thunder, Lightning, thank you. You two were great. The rest of you, not so much."

Peering into the room from the hallway, Parasite, the janitor, grumbled. He knew who'd be cleaning up the mess.

Inside, The Flash looked down at his feet. Beast Boy turned into a mouse. Bumblebee took her seat and leaned forward, ready to hear what the teacher had to say.

"Today's class was about weather manipulation and how we can circumvent potential natural disasters," Lucius Fox told them. "Do you know what the number one thing most of you did wrong was?"

Harley was waving her hand high in the air. "Ask me! Ask me!"

Mr. Fox peered over his glasses. "Ms. Quinn, what was the number one thing most of you did wrong?"

Harley tugged on one of her ponytails. "One thing?" she said with a broad smile. "**WOWZA**, there are soooo many choices. Who can choose just one?"

As Harley began counting on her fingers and listing things like "shoulda worn my new galoshes," "shoulda checked the weather," and "shoulda eaten more snacks for energy," the teacher shook his head. "Anyone else?" he asked.

Bumblebee thought for a moment, then nodded ever so slightly.

"Yes, Bumblebee?" Mr. Fox said.

"You gave us time to think about what was happening," she began, "but when we got the signal to go, we all just dove right in."

The teacher pointed at Bumblebee. "She's on to something," he said excitedly. "Who else?"

Wonder Woman raised her hand. "We had time to talk to each other, to formulate a plan. But instead, we all just acted on our own."

Katana was next. "And we are stronger as a team than as individuals."

"Now you're getting it," Mr. Fox said, nodding. "Yes, Harley?"

"We shoulda worked together!" she said, proud of herself for having just thought of it. As the room broke into laughter, Harley looked around. "What's so funny? Did I miss something?"

"I'll tell you later," Bumblebee assured her as the bell for the next class rang.

Red Tornado was an imposing figure. A massive red robot, he was an expert when it came to flight training and took it very seriously, as did most of his students. The only time anyone had seen him flustered was when Queen Hippolyta, Wonder Woman's mom, had shown up at school one day and said hello to him.

Bumblebee checked her wings. Light and aerodynamic, they were surprisingly strong. She had been practicing free-falling, then swooping upward just inches before she hit the ground, allowing the power boost from her super suit to propel her higher.

Beast Boy had turned into a pterodactyl, a prehistoric flying reptile with an impressive wingspan and a menacing beak. As he flapped his wings, the drawings Katana had been making of her classmates scattered. "Hey, watch where you're flying!" she said.

Non-flyers were also required to take flight training. As Red Tornado put it, "There are times when you will need to know how your opponent operates in flight. That way, you can use your own unique powers to counteract their advantage."

Miss Martian hurried over to help Katana gather her papers. Beast Boy had turned into an octopus and was using all eight arms to gather the drawings. "Sorry! Sorry!" he kept saying. But the papers kept ripping when anyone tried to pull them free from his suckers, which just made things worse.

"Beast Boy!" Katana cried, startling him. "Ooooh, no," she said when she saw what had just happened.

"Oh, wow," Beast Boy octopus said apologetically. "But you know what happens when an octopus startles, right?"

Miss Martian said softly, "It squirts ink."

Katana's drawings were ruined.

As Beast Boy begged for Katana's forgiveness, Bumblebee tried not to laugh. It was never dull at Super Hero High.

"Attention, class!" Red Tornado bellowed. "Stop goofing off. We have work to do."

Instantly, the Supers were standing in a straight row, arms behind their backs, listening to their teacher. Even Beast Boy.

"Today we are going to tackle natural disasters," Red Tornado said, beaming a list onto the wall. "That means learning how to navigate through all kinds of unfriendly conditions, including hurricanes, tornadoes, earthquakes, and tsunamis. Wonder Woman and Hawkgirl, you're up. Class, watch and learn. We're going to start by creating an avalanche."

He nodded at Frost. She raised her hands over her head and began to make a mountain of snow and ice that got bigger and bigger and bigger. . . .

CHAPTER 5

"**W**ell, that was a disaster," Hawkgirl was saying as she adjusted her Nth Metal belt and flapped her wings to remove the excess ice.

"And there was nothing natural about it," quipped Harley.

"I thought it was sort of fun," said Wonder Woman, brushing the snow off her golden shield.

"I did my part and created the snow and ice," Frost said defensively. Her cool blue hair was pulled up into a ponytail on top of her head, making it look like a cascade of sleek, shiny ice was falling down her back. "It's not my fault that you two couldn't get the avalanche to go in the right direction."

Wonder Woman and Hawkgirl glanced at each other.

"Well," Poison Ivy said, wanting to head off an argument between her friends, "the good news is that before it did permanent damage to the school grounds, El Diablo was able to melt the snow, and then Supergirl created irrigation ditches so that the runoff could water the cornfield I'm growing."

"It made for great video," Harley added. "Especially when it looked like the school was about to get buried in snow."

"You posted that already?" asked Bumblebee. Harley never ceased to amaze her. A lot of kids at Super Hero High were like that—doing the seemingly impossible. But then, what did you expect from a school of the best of the best? Sometimes she couldn't even believe she went to Super Hero High.

"Posted it the sec I got out of class," boasted Harley. She did a vault over Hawkgirl's chair, followed by a cartwheel, and landed on top of her desk with her hands raised in the air. No one blinked. They were used to it.

The woman in the front of the room with the blond hair and a bell on her sweater shook her head. "Harley Quinn," their teacher, Liberty Belle, cautioned, "we've talked about this before. Save your gymnastics for Coach Wildcat's P.E. class. In Super Hero History, you'll learn best by sitting down and looking up front."

Batgirl turned on her new Scribble Scrawler, a mini-computer she had designed that translated handwriting into type and then automatically organized it, adding footnotes and citations. Big Barda gripped a pen. She had a dozen more at the ready, since she tended to press too hard when she wrote and often broke them. Poison Ivy whispered to the Candytuft flowers in her backpack.

"Ivy," Liberty Belle said gently. "No talking to your plants in class."

Poison Ivy sat up, her face turning the color of her red hair. "Sorry," she said. "It's just that I'm training my Candytuft flowers to listen and play back what they hear."

Liberty Belle nodded. "In that case, fine," she said, then turned to the class. "I know you've been studying natural disasters with your other teachers," she began. "So I've decided to continue this trend by going over some of the more famous incidents in history. Who can name a catastrophic natural disaster?"

Lots of hands were raised. There were the usual—Wonder Woman, Batgirl, and Hawkgirl. Liberty Belle scanned the room. "Big Barda," she said brightly. "Let's hear from you."

Barda looked around. Frost and Cheetah were whispering to each other and giggling. "On my home planet, Apokolips, there was a huge earthquake," Barda began. She shut her eyes, remembering it. "The ground shook so hard that everyone was tossed around, slamming into walls, toppling off bridges. I was little when it happened, but I can still remember the devastation. Buildings fell and whole towns were destroyed, and they were never rebuilt even though Darkseid, our ruler, promised they would be."

When she opened her eyes, everyone was staring at her. Barda pressed her lips together and said softly, "Um . . . earthquakes are a type of natural disaster."

"So are villains who pretend to be super heroes," someone who sounded suspiciously like Frost said loud enough to be heard by some, but soft enough for the teacher not to notice.

"Big Barda is a true super hero," Supergirl said, shushing Frost.

"And she has fought bravely in battle," Wonder Woman added.

"I challenge anyone to prove otherwise!" Supergirl exclaimed.

Liberty Belle cleared her throat loudly. The room went silent. The teacher said, "Thank you for sharing a firsthand experience, Barda. That must have been very hard to do. I appreciate it."

Big Barda nodded and looked at Supergirl, who gave her a warm smile. Everyone knew that Barda had once tried to overthrow Super Hero High, but it seemed like a long time ago. Since then, she had changed her ways, and she was now one of the school's most loyal students.

Barda smiled back at Supergirl as their teacher continued.

"Now, class, we are going to learn about Earth's natural disasters, then discuss what we could have done to help, had we been there. Let's start with the Lake Nyos limnic eruption. Does anyone know what that was? Yes, Batgirl?"

"Limnic eruptions are rare, and this one occurred in a lake in the Cameroonian jungle," Batgirl began. "A magma chamber leaked carbon dioxide into the water, changing it to carbonic acid and causing the lake to erupt."

"Excellent research!" Liberty Belle exclaimed. "Now, who can tell us how we could have prevented this?"

Raven raised her hand. Her ruby-red lipstick matched the red gem on her forehead. Bumblebee admired her short, dark hair with red tips. She had thought about cutting her hair that short, or even getting a buzz cut, but in the end decided she liked her long, wavy hair. "It couldn't have been prevented," Raven said. "I've been to places like that, and it would be nearly impossible to monitor them all."

"We could try, couldn't we?" asked Miss Martian meekly.

"That would be difficult," Liberty Belle said as Miss Martian began to fade from sight. "Though it's a great idea. However, on Earth, there are around 117 million lakes."

"So what do we do?" Bumblebee asked. One hundred and seventeen million was a lot.

"I was just about to ask all of you that very same question," said Liberty Belle. "You will pair up alphabetically. Each team will have twenty minutes to come up with a solution. Batgirl and Barda, you're a team. Beast Boy, you're with Bumblebee. Cheetah and Cyborg—"

Bumblebee would have rather been partnered with Poison Ivy, or Batgirl, or *anyone* but Beast Boy. He was so annoying!

Now, as she glanced at him, he morphed into a frog, then a rabbit, and then a skunk.

"Can you please just settle on one animal—except the skunk—so we can focus on our assignment?" Bumblebee asked him. She prided herself on getting things done quickly and efficiently. That was probably why Principal Waller had handpicked Bumblebee as one of her office aides.

"Aw, okay. Fine," Beast Boy said, settling on being himself.

"Thank you," said Bumblebee. "Now, let's start with the givens."

"The Givens?" Beast Boy asked. "Who are they?"

Bumblebee wasn't sure if he was serious or teasing her. " 'The givens' means the facts," she explained.

Her partner burst out laughing. "I knew that," he said, nudging her and rolling his eyes. "Duh!"

Bumblebee tried not to fume. As the twenty minutes rushed by, Beast Boy seemed to have a joke for whatever she said. "Don't you take anything seriously?" she asked.

He grinned and raised both hands in the air as if to surrender. But before he could reply, Liberty Belle called out, "Time's up! Beast Boy, you're raising your hands. Does that mean you and Bumblebee would like to go first?"

CHAPTER 6

"**W**e would be happy to go first!" Beast Boy said as he ran to the front of the room. "Isn't that right, partner?"

Bumblebee sat rooted to her chair with her arms crossed. For a brief second, she had allowed her mind to wander back to the fact that her house had been destroyed. Since she had seen the ruins, Bumblebee couldn't stop thinking about it. But school assignments, homework, and being a part-time assistant to Principal Waller kept her busy—not to mention that here she was, in class with Beast Boy as a partner. He had contributed *zero* ideas to the project! If anything, he was a total distraction. And now he was volunteering them to go first?

"What's the matter?" Beast Boy asked, unaware that she was fuming again. "C'mon, you slowpoke!"

Liberty Belle said encouragingly, "I'm looking forward to hearing what you have come up with."

"Sure thing!" Beast Boy said as Bumblebee dragged

herself to the front of the room. Beast Boy smiled at his partner. "Go on, tell them our brilliant plan, Bumblebee!" When she glared at him, he leaned in and whispered, "Make it good. I need to bring my grade up in this class!"

"It would be nearly impossible to monitor all 117 million lakes," Bumblebee began through gritted teeth.

"Impossible!" shouted Beast Boy.

Ignoring him, she went on, "The best thing we can do is to have a rescue plan in place. . . ."

"Rescue plan!" he began chanting. "Rescue plan! Rescue plan!"

Bumblebee refused to even look at Beast Boy. "With a rescue plan," she continued, "everyone knows what their job is, and that way we can respond immediately at the first sign of a limnic eruption."

"Limnic! Limnic! Limnic!" Beast Boy broke into a little dance.

As she went on, Beast Boy kept nodding and repeating random words she had just said. When Bumblebee was done, he led the room in applause. "And that's what we came up with," he said, taking a bow. "The two of us. Both. Her and me. Me and she. Him and her, and her and him—"

"Thank you, Bumblebee," Liberty Belle said, giving her a knowing look, ". . . and Beast Boy."

"We make a great team, don't you think?" Beast Boy was trying to keep up with Bumblebee, who was walking faster and faster to get away from his annoying presence. Finally, she shrank to the size of a bee and began to fly. Undaunted, Beast Boy turned into a hummingbird and flew alongside her.

"I can't talk now," she said, brushing him aside. "I have to go to Principal Waller's office."

"In trouble again?" he joked. Everyone knew that Bumblebee never got in trouble. If anything, teachers were always holding her up as an example of a good student, which made some kids jealous.

"You coming or not?" Bumblebee asked innocently as she turned full-sized and opened the door. She knew that Beast Boy dreaded walking into the principal's office, having been sent there way too many times.

"Or not!" he answered, turning into a small green gecko and scurrying away.

CHAPTER 7

When Bumblebee walked into the administration office, she noted the huge pile of mail on the counter. From the principal's office off to the side, Amanda Waller looked up and said, "Close my door, please." She covered the phone with her hand. "I need some privacy."

Bumblebee shut the door and began sorting the mail. It was her job to answer questions, deliver messages, and assist the principal. There were other office aides, one student per class period. But Waller often saved the more complicated or confidential work for Bumblebee.

Though the door was shut, Bumblebee could still hear Amanda Waller's booming voice. Always an imposing presence, the principal was famous for her strict no-nonsense approach to leadership, her stern demeanor, and her steadfast allegiance to her students. The Supers were loyal to her, as well. They knew that Super Hero High students were selected not based on who they were today, but, as their principal always said, "on who they could become tomorrow." She gave everyone a chance to prove themselves—Bumblebee included.

"Natural disasters . . ." Bumblebee couldn't help but overhear Waller talking. "An increasing number . . ."

That weekend, there was a surprise for everyone. Supergirl led her friends to the outskirts of Super Hero High to Poison Ivy's cornfield, where she had whimsically arranged the rows of corn so that they formed an incredible maze. As the Supers merrily weaved in and out of the tall green stalks, Supergirl could be heard reminding her very competitive friends, "No fair flying. Everyone needs to stay on the ground!"

Bumblebee explained to Barda as they ran, "A lot of the grain crops, like corn, wheat, and rice, rely on the wind or are self-pollinating. Insects and birds also help pollinate, but bees are the most famous for it."

"Hurry!" Poison Ivy called out at the end of the maze. "There's more."

As everyone gathered around, Supergirl said, "You're all invited to my Aunt Martha and Uncle Jonathan's farm for a big feast. But first, this!"

Supergirl took flight and, using her heat vision, ignited the cornstalks and their husks, which wrapped around rich yellow kernels of corn. Cheers erupted as it began to rain . . . popcorn!

Cheetah and Frost helped Poison Ivy pass out hundreds of paper bags with the Super Hero High logo on them, and everyone began filling them up. Then the Supers delivered them to citizens in Metropolis's Centennial Park, residents at Fountain of Youth senior citizens' home, and guests at the First Annual Foodie Fair. And when they were done, there was plenty left over for them.

Batgirl added Parmesan cheese to her popcorn, Cheetah sprinkled shredded coconut on hers, and Bumblebee poured honey over hers.

That evening, several Supers headed to Smallville, where they gathered at the Kent family farm. When Supergirl had first come to Earth after her home planet had been destroyed, Martha and Jonathan Kent had taken her in. Now that she was at Super Hero High, the Kents loved nothing more than to have her come to the farm and bring her friends.

As always, there was a home-cooked feast—crispy golden fried chicken, a colorful medley of roasted vegetables, three kinds of salads, mashed potatoes, and plenty of BBQ. The Supers appreciated this, since their families were often far away, sometimes even on other planets, busy working as super heroes themselves. Sadly, in some cases, there were teens without parents. They were casualties in the battle against evil.

After dinner, Katana used her mighty sword to split wood for a bonfire. "Three . . . two . . . one . . . ," the Supers shouted in unison. "NOW!"

With that, using her heat vision, Supergirl lit the woodpile up in flames. After the cheers, the Supers gathered around, roasting marshmallows and making s'mores with graham crackers dusted with cinnamon sugar and thick bars of chocolate.

"I had planned on serving home-baked peach pies," Aunt Martha said. She wiped her hands on her apron as she admired the crackling bonfire. "But for some reason, our peach crop didn't come in as well as we had hoped this year."

"The meal was wonderful, thank you," Bumblebee said. Her stomach hurt a bit from eating so much, but it was worth it. "I'm sure the peach pie would have been great, too. But I'm just happy to be here."

"You're welcome," said Aunt Martha. "The peaches—it's the darnedest thing. Usually they come in juicy and ripe and incredibly sweet. But this year . . . Oh well. I'm sure there's a good explanation for it. . . ."

CHAPTER 8

Taking a break between classes was one of Bumblebee's favorite parts of the day. And to the young hero's way of thinking, any time was a good time for a honey break!

Katana was already seated and slicing lemons—occasionally cutting some into pleasing shapes. "And now for a sunflower," she said while Poison Ivy looked on approvingly. Everyone loved how Katana could use her swords to battle the most vicious villains *and* to add that little extra oomph to tea time.

Wonder Woman was pouring each of her friends a cup of hot tea. She took a deep breath as steam lifted the delicate scent to her nose.

Bumblebee looked at her cup. Something was missing. She rummaged around in her backpack and pulled out a bottle that gave off a warm golden glow. It was shaped like the super-villain Granny Goodness, and the eyes on the bottle bugged out a little every time she squeezed it.

Supergirl raised an eyebrow. "I thought we'd seen the last of her," she said, recalling the battle between the Supers and Granny's army of Female Furies.

Bumblebee laughed. "This is from one of my fans—you know, the Honey Bees."

Batgirl nodded. "Thought so," she said. "They're always sending you honey! You're so lucky. My fan club usually sends me computer problems they want me to fix."

"Can I see that?" Big Barda reached for the Granny Goodness honey. She squeezed it hard, emptying all the honey into her tea so that the cup overflowed. "That's more like it," she said.

Laughter rang out. Everyone knew that the evil Granny Goodness was Barda's former mentor. Giving her a squeeze must have been like sweet revenge for Barda.

"Here, have more!" Bumblebee said, tossing Barda another Granny Goodness-shaped honey bottle. "There's lots more where that came from."

Mr. and Ms. Andrena-Beecher had been checking in with their daughter on a regular basis from their relative's house. "We saw you on *Harley's Quinntessentials,*" her father said proudly. "That Harley sure has a lot of energy."

Bumblebee had recently been featured on Harley Quinn's

web channel. Since her battery pack was having problems holding a charge, Bumblebee had been walking, instead of flying, to Capes & Cowls Café. That was when Scooter, a little boy, had run up to her. "Save Rainbow!" he had cried, pointing up.

Perched lazily on a top branch of a nearby tree was Rainbow the cat. Famous for getting stuck up trees, she now had her own popular segment, "Save Rainbow!"

"I'm not sure Rainbow wants to be saved," Bumblebee said.

"Save Rainbow!" Scooter said tearfully. "It's time for her lunch."

Reluctantly, Bumblebee got bee-sized and flew up to the wayward cat, knowing that when she was that small, she had a better chance of getting Rainbow to get down on her own.

"Hi, kitty," Bumblebee said. "What's up?"

Rainbow looked bored and meowed. Lazily, she swatted at a bee slowly buzzing by. Noticing more bees Bumblebee nodded to Rainbow. "Hey, bee pals!" she called out. "How's it going?"

To her surprise, not only did the bees ignore her, but they also seemed lethargic. A few even appeared to fall asleep mid-flight and dropped to the ground.

"Hey, I gotta go check on them," Bumblebee said to Rainbow. "You need to get down on your own. I'm not going to carry you. You can do it."

Rainbow didn't understand her, or at least was pretending not to. "Scooter's waiting for you, and he's upset," Bumblebee explained. "He's got your lunch." She paused, then added, "But if you don't want it, I'm sure he can find another cat who does."

Rainbow flattened her ears in surprise, then scrambled down the tree.

As Harley had interviewed a tearfully happy Scooter, who was clutching Rainbow, Bumblebee had flown to the beehive. Normally busy and buzzing, it had been strangely silent. The bees on the ground had still been alive, but it was as if they were in a deep sleep. She hadn't known what to make of it.

"Save Rainbow!" her father yelled over the phone, bringing her back to the present.

"We love seeing you on *Harley's Quinntessentials* and FaceTalking with you," her mother added. "So how are things?"

"Things are fine," Bumblebee informed them. "I need to finish that upgrade on my battle suit—especially the new battery pack—but it's hard not having my own lab. How are you two? How's the house rehab going?"

"Longer than we'd like," her mother confessed. "And I don't want to overstay our welcome at Cousin Keisha's."

"They're driving each other crazy," Mr. Andrena-Beecher cut in.

His wife playfully swatted him. "That's not true," she

said, laughing. Then she added, "Well, maybe a little."

Bumblebee joined in the laughter. She knew what it was like when someone overstayed their welcome. Liberty Belle had decided to extend the natural disaster topic and turn it into a full-fledged project. "You will stay with your original partners," she had informed the class. Which meant two words that Bumblebee would have rather not had to deal with: *Beast Boy*.

"It's gonna be fun! It's gonna be great! It's gonna be Beast Boy and Bumblebee all the way," he had said as he changed into a mosquito and buzzed around her. Bumblebee had tried to ignore him.

Now she joked, "I wonder if there's room at Cousin Keisha's for Beast Boy."

"I thought you liked Beast Boy," her mother said.

"He's okay in small doses," Bumblebee said, adding, "Very small."

"Bumblebee!" Principal Waller called out later that afternoon. Instantly, Bumblebee was in her office. "Please tell Coach Wildcat that I want everyone to be in peak form," Waller said.

"But aren't we always supposed to be in peak form?" Bumblebee asked. She covered her mouth as the words came out. It was a risk to question the principal.

Waller narrowed her eyes. Bumblebee tried not to tremble. She had faced down villains, fought in epic battles, and endured physical hardships, but all paled against the stern look that Amanda Waller was capable of.

"You're right," the principal said, nodding. "Tell Wildcat I want everyone in peak form—and by peak, I mean higher than the top of the Himalayas."

Bumblebee exhaled. "Will do, Principal Waller," she said, practically singing. She was so relieved. "I'm on it."

CHAPTER 9

Coach Wildcat adjusted his baseball cap as he glared at his students. Many had just finished running twenty miles, doing one hundred one-finger pushups, and lifting cars.

"Who here thinks they are in great shape?" he asked.

Wonder Woman raised her hand.

He nodded to her, then continued. "Well, we can always be better," he said. When no one responded, he yelled, "Am I right, or am I right?"

"You are right!" the class yelled back in unison.

Bumblebee was always striving to do better. She was keenly aware that she was not as naturally strong as Supergirl, or as adept at aiming her sonic blasts as Arrowette was at aiming her arrows, or nearly as fast as The Flash. But when she wore her battle suit, Bumblebee's reflexes, speed, and strength were greatly enhanced. Plus, it gave her the power of flight, the ability to emit sonic blasts, and, most importantly, the ability to shrink to the size of a bee.

"Bigger is not always better," her mother used to say. Lately, though, Bumblebee had noticed that her strength and stamina had been waning. If only she still had her backup suit. But all was lost when the Bee Tree Lab fell.

Bumblebee watched her fellow Supers exerting their strength, battling each other, and testing their limits. Normally, she wouldn't have hesitated to join in. But today, she could feel her battery draining. Who was she without her super suit? Bumblebee began to wonder. Oh, sure, there were several Supers at Super Hero High who weren't born with powers but who acquired them along the way, or who had rings or weapons that gave them their enhanced abilities. And there were others who were just, well, super no matter what, like Cheetah. Bumblebee had always admired her strength and confidence. Cheetah never seemed to doubt herself—and that alone seemed like a superpower.

When Bumblebee turned the corner, there were a few students gathered around the community bulletin board. On it were flyers for clubs—AT THE KNITTING AND HITTING CLUB YOU CAN DO BOTH . . . AT THE SAME TIME! —and flyers for volunteer opportunities—NEEDED: FOUR SUPERS TO ASSIST IN CLEANING THE OCEAN. SWIMMERS AND FLYERS PREFERRED, BUT ALL WELCOME—and flyers for things gone missing—LOST: ONE TUBE OF DARK RED LIPSTICK. IF FOUND,

SEE RAVEN. BIG REWARD.

Bumblebee was about to turn away when something caught her eye. It was a nondescript flyer that read HAVING AN IDENTITY CRISIS? QUESTIONING YOUR LIFE? FEEL LIKE AN IMPOSTER? SIGN UP TO SEE DR. ARKHAM TODAY!

CHAPTER 10

"Ah, Ms. Bumblebee!" Dr. Arkham called out. "Come in, come in! Do you have an extremely important and confidential missive for me from Amanda Waller?"

Bumblebee entered the school counselor's office. She didn't spend much time here aside from delivering messages from Principal Waller, or for her annual assessment. All Supers had to have one. It was imperative that they be not only physically fit but mentally fit. Being a super hero was no easy job.

"Not this time," she said, sounding apologetic. "I have an eight-thirty appointment." Bumblebee wished she had something more important than her worries to bring to Dr. Arkham this early in the morning.

As she looked around the room, she noticed that he had a fireplace mantel but no fireplace. On the mantel were framed pictures of Dr. Arkham at various ages, ending up with a recent one showcasing his magnificently bald head, well-groomed beard, and befuddled stare.

"Do you think I should have smiled more?" Dr. Arkham asked, looking serious.

"No, oh no," she assured him. "This picture is terrific just as it is. It looks just like you."

"Well, thank you, Bumblebee," he said, looking pleased. "Now, what are we here to talk about today?"

It was hard at first. Bumblebee wasn't like Harley, who spoke before thinking, and she wasn't like Hawkgirl, who sounded like she had practiced what she was going to say. And she certainly wasn't like Beast Boy, who just never stopped talking.

"I saw your flyer, the one about feeling like an imposter," Bumblebee began.

Arkham nodded knowingly. "Ah, yes. The imposter syndrome affects lots of high achievers, and I daresay this school is full of them. People with the syndrome fear that their success may not be warranted, despite evidence to the contrary. They have trouble accepting their accomplishments, dismissing them as luck or timing. They sometimes think they are fooling people into believing that they are something they are not."

Dr. Arkham lowered his glasses. "Do you know anyone like this?"

Bumblebee wondered if he was reading her mind, like

Miss Martian. That was *exactly* how she felt at times.

"Maybe," she confessed. "I used to play super hero so much when I was little that now that I'm actually here, I can't help but think I'm pretending to be someone I'm not. If I were a true super hero, wouldn't I have been able to save my parents' house?"

Bumblebee's eyes began to water. She reached for a tissue. Dr. Arkham had several boxes scattered all around his office. He was famous for buying cases of tissues whenever they were on sale.

She went on, "I know that Principal Waller always says we were accepted here not based on who we are today, but who we can become tomorrow, but what if I'm not who everyone thinks I am? What if I'm not really Bumblebee, but just little Karen Andrena-Beecher, pretending to be a super hero?"

Dr. Arkham nodded. "That's for you to decide, Bumblebee. The only person in charge of your destiny is *you*!" He coughed, then confessed, "I read that on a coffee mug."

Bumblebee nodded. "So you're saying that I'm the one to determine my fate. That it's up to me to make things happen, not just wait around and wait for life to lead me? But that I must be present, and more than that, I need to be accountable for my actions and reactions, and accept my successes as well as my failures?"

"Whoa! That sounds excellent. Let me write that down," Arkham said, nodding enthusiastically. "I wonder if that would fit on a coffee mug?"

"Thank you, Dr. Arkham!" Bumblebee said. She felt better already.

"Before you leave, I'll let you in on a secret," he said, leaning forward. "One of the greatest minds here at Super Hero High had the imposter syndrome. This amazing person was afraid of being found out to be a fake, a pretender, and didn't trust their own accomplishments. But they later learned to embrace all that they had to offer the world."

Bumblebee's eyes grew wide. "Who?" she asked.

"Me!" Arkham said, beaming. "Now, can you tell the next student to come in, please?"

As she exited, Bumblebee was surprised to see that a line had formed outside the door. "I guess you're next," she told Wonder Woman.

CHAPTER 11

"So I'm working on a Bat-Netspray," Batgirl explained enthusiastically. "One that'll spray a net over a bad guy, then harden so they can't escape. So far, it's working great. See?"

Bumblebee looked over at Beast Boy, who was crouched in a corner with a hard-shell net over him. He smiled and waved.

They were in the Bat-Bunker. The walls matched the purple on Batgirl's costume. Bumblebee noted that the room was much darker than the Bee Tree Lab. The lab had always been flooded with sunlight during the day and lit up by voice-activated lights at night. But Bumblebee supposed that Batgirl needed the dark to make her dozens of computer screens illuminate all the better.

"Now that your lab is gone, what's happening with all your projects?" Batgirl asked.

Bumblebee glanced at one of the monitors. It looked like Batgirl was tracking a storm system.

"Nothing's going on," she said glumly.

"Weren't you working on a new super suit?" Batgirl asked.

Bumblebee walked over to Beast Boy and gave the strands of the net a pull. Batgirl hadn't quite figured out yet how to release whoever was in her trap. "Is he stuck in there forever?" Bumblebee teased.

"I'd better not be!" Beast Boy exclaimed. "I got places to go, people to meet, jokes to make!"

Bumblebee looked over Batgirl's shoulder at the 3-D model on the screen. "What are you working on?" she asked.

"Besides setting Beast Boy free, I'm also helping Cyborg create a stronger metal that not only deflects lasers, but then redirects them back to their source," Batgirl said.

Bumblebee nodded as she tried to build up her courage. There was something she had been wanting to ask her friend. "Say, Batgirl," Bumblebee began hesitantly. "I was wondering if I could use your lab now and then. But only until mine is rebuilt," she quickly added.

"What was that?" Batgirl asked. She swiveled her chair around to face Bumblebee.

"She wants to use your lab!" Beast Boy yelled. "Maybe Bumblebee can get me out of here!"

"My lab, the Bat-Bunker?" Batgirl asked. She looked stricken.

Bumblebee felt awful. It was probably too much to

have asked. "Never mind," she said quickly. She was glad it was dark in the room so that Batgirl couldn't see how embarrassed she was.

"And . . . awkward silence!" Beast Boy shouted.

"Oh, Bumblebee!" Batgirl said. "I am so embarrassed. I should have offered my lab to you the minute I found out about the Bee Tree Lab being destroyed. What kind of friend am I?"

"Apparently not a very good one," Beast Boy quipped as he continued to strain against his bonds.

"Bumblebee, please," Batgirl continued. "I would like nothing more than to share the Bat-Bunker with you!"

A smile lit up Bumblebee's face. Batgirl would do that for her? As if reading her mind, Batgirl added, "After all, I know you'd do the same for me."

Bumblebee nodded. That was true. "Thank you!" she said, rushing to give her a hug.

As the girls chatted nonstop about how much fun they'd have working side by side, Beast Boy called out, "Ahem! Hey! What about me? Hello! I'm still here!"

Bumblebee let out an exasperated sigh. "You know," she said, "you could just turn yourself into something small if you *really* wanted out."

Beast Boy's green cheeks flushed a deeper shade of green. "I knew that," he said unconvincingly. He transformed into a wasp and buzzed free of the netting. "I just wanted to see how long it would take *you* to figure it out."

"What's mine is yours," Batgirl said cheerfully. It was the third day of Bumblebee's sharing the Bat-Bunker. "Take whatever you need." She returned to the 3-D image of Cyborg with lasers aimed at him.

Bumblebee lingered over Batgirl's worktable. Everything was neatly organized, unlike in her lab, where her equipment had always lain scattered about. One time when her mom had asked, "Have you ever given any thought to organizing the Bee Tree Lab?" Bumblebee truly hadn't known what she was talking about.

Though her lab may have looked sloppy, it was anything but that. Bumblebee's analytical mind cataloged all her equipment, plus the status of her projects and what the next steps were. Everyone knew that when Principal Waller couldn't find a missing file, her coffee mug, or a recently confiscated super weapon, Bumblebee was the first person she asked to help her.

Bumblebee picked up the hydraulic torque wrench, a handful of titanium cubes, and a small solar vial. "What's all this?" she asked Batgirl.

"Oh, just something I'm working on for Poison Ivy," Batgirl replied. "I'm trying to capture sunlight and turn it into liquid energy. She wants to be able to sprinkle it on her plants during overcast days."

"Sunshine in a jar!" Bumblebee said, tucking away the information. She waved the wrench in the air. "This will do for now," she said as she powered down her super suit.

Bumblebee needed to conserve energy. With only one super suit, she couldn't afford to burn it out. Yet it seemed she was doing just that. Her battery pack was draining at an alarming rate and had to be constantly recharged.

As the two friends worked in silence, each on her own project, Bumblebee observed Batgirl. She seemed so confident, like nothing ever fazed her. Even though Bumblebee had felt buoyed when leaving Dr. Arkham's office, she still had her doubts.

CHAPTER 12

Since Batgirl had the most computers, everyone gathered in the Bat-Bunker. There was excitement in the air as she flipped a switch and all her computer screens began broadcasting Harley's web channel.

"Up soon, a brand-new show!!!" Harley shouted online. "But first, this!"

The Supers were treated to a scene of The Flash running so fast that he miscalculated the edge of a cliff and fell off—only to be rescued by Wonder Woman, flying by in her Invisible Jet. Cheers went up as Wonder Woman tossed her Lasso of Truth to The Flash, who grabbed it with one hand and waved happily at the camera with the other as he was pulled back to school.

In the Bat-Bunker, The Flash stood up and pointed to himself on-screen, then bowed to his friends. "To Wonder Woman!" he cheered.

Wonder Woman smiled back. She was passing out

tumblers of fresh-squeezed lemonade and Frost was blowing on them to turn them into slushies. "Cookies?" Supergirl was saying as she circled the room. "They're from Aunt Martha."

"Any honey snickerdoodles?" Bumblebee asked.

Supergirl used her X-ray vision to assess the basket piled high with fresh baked treats. "Doesn't look like it," she said. "Aunt Martha said she wasn't able to get all of her regular ingredients. But here, try this ginger molasses one."

Bumblebee bit in. The cookie was crispy on the edges and chewy in the middle, and the spiced ginger and cinnamon were complemented by the coarse granulated sugar generously sprinkled on top. "Mmmm, thank you!" she said as Supergirl handed Harley a chocolate and vanilla pinwheel cookie.

"*WOWZA!* This is making me dizzy," Harley quipped as she spun her cookie around on the tip of her finger while doing a series of flips.

"What about you, Poison Ivy?" Bumblebee asked. "Aren't you having any cookies?"

Ivy tried to force a smile. "I'm too nervous to eat," she admitted.

"Nervous, schmervous!" Harley said, biting around and around her cookie in the pinwheel pattern. "You were great. You'll see. *Quiet, everyone!* The show's about to begin. Oh, look, it's me on the screens!"

The Supers crowded around the computers once again

as they were treated to the new theme music. "Today we're gonna see a **YOWZA** of a new show," Harley exclaimed, looking straight at the camera. "Yes! It's the debut of *Harley's Greenhouse Hullabaloo,* starring Super Hero High's very own . . . Poison Ivy!"

Everyone started clapping. Only Bumblebee noticed Poison Ivy back into a dark corner of the Bat-Bunker. There, she leaned against the wall, then slid down so she was sitting on the floor, hugging her knees.

"Hello, Poison Ivy," Harley was saying to the camera as she held a microphone in front of Ivy's face. "For those few who have never heard of you, tell them who you are!"

Poison Ivy looked stiff as she leaned into the mic and said in a soft voice, "Um. Er, my name is Poison Ivy."

"We know that," Harley whispered, then winked at the camera. "Tell us about yourself."

Unblinking, Ivy stared at the camera. The room hushed in an effort to hear her. "I'm Ivy and I like science and plants and I grow things and do experiments and I have red hair," she said on one breath.

"YIKES! That's awesome sauce!" shouted Harley. "And luckily for you *Harley's Quinntessentials* viewers, Poison Ivy is the host for the *Greenhouse Hullabaloo.* Ivy, tell them about it!"

Poison Ivy gulped and then leaned into the microphone

again. "Um, Supergirl and Hawkgirl and lots of others from Super Hero High helped create a mega greenhouse."

"Speak up," Harley said.

"A MEGA GREENHOUSE!" shouted Ivy, startling herself. She blinked rapidly before continuing, looking uncomfortable and miserable at the same time. "It has room for multiple environments. I'll be growing lots of familiar and exotic plants in here"—the camera pulled back to reveal a greenhouse the size of a football stadium—"and will also be interviewing some of the world's best gardeners."

In her enthusiasm, Harley nudged her a little too hard and sent her sprawling onto the ground outside of camera range. Poison Ivy got up and brushed herself off, and came back on-screen just in time to look left, at her first guest. Standing there with a blissful smile and a head of thick white hair punctuated by streaks of black was Abby Holland, plant enthusiast and contributor to *Beautiful Blossoms* magazine.

Abby was wearing a cape made entirely of hothouse flowers—colorful orchids, majestic birds-of-paradise, and flamingo lily anthuriums. It was *not* her usual style, but Harley had insisted she wear it, claiming that the down-to-earth Abby needed more flash and pizzazz. "Abby, you look great. The camera is going to love you," Harley announced as she backflipped away. "Okay, Ivy, the show's all yours!"

On the computer screen, Poison Ivy stood frozen with

Abby Holland at her side. Neither spoke. The Flash coughed into his hand to help diffuse the discomfort in the room. Supergirl asked if anyone would like more of her Aunt Martha's cookies. Beast Boy started fidgeting.

"Quiet. Quiet! QUIET!" Harley yelled. "Watch what happens next!"

On the screen, a look of determination washed over Ivy's face. She stopped slouching, stood tall, and took a deep breath as she gripped the microphone. "So, tell me, Abby Holland," she began softly. "What can you share with us about the world's most beautiful flowers?"

With that, Abby lit up and began showcasing all the varieties of flowers she had brought with her. As they talked flowers, Ivy loosened up, asking questions, adding fun facts, and admiring all that Abby Holland had brought to the greenhouse. At the end, Abby declared, "I'm leaving all these rare potted Semper Augustus tulips, my personal faves, with you so that you can give them a home here."

For the first time since the show started, Ivy looked genuinely happy. "Thank you!" she said, waving at the flowers. Some waved back at her. Then Poison Ivy turned to the camera, as if suddenly remembering it was there. Her posture and voice became more robotic. "This is Poison Ivy signing off from *Harley's Greenhouse Hullabaloo*. Join me next week as I interview more famous gardeners, and *I'll* show *you* what's growing in the greenhouse."

As the room erupted in applause, Batgirl turned off the monitors. "That was wonderful, Ivy," Katana said, looking around. "Poison Ivy?"

Bumblebee had made herself small and followed Ivy as she snuck out of the Bat-Bunker just before the segment ended.

"Are you okay?" she asked. Poison Ivy was sitting under a blossoming cherry tree inside the greenhouse on the outskirts of campus.

Ivy wiped a tear away and pretended she had something in her eye. "I was awful," she said, choking back her sobs. "That was so embarrassing."

"You weren't awful, and it wasn't as bad as you thought," said Bumblebee. "I know Harley can be . . . well, let's put it this way: Harley is very good at convincing people to do things. If you feel that hosting the show is something you'd rather not do, you don't have to. But *really*—you were doing great by the end."

Ivy looked around the massive greenhouse. Unlike a hothouse warmed by artificial sources, the greenhouse was heated solely by the sun that streamed through its glass enclosure. However, Ivy had placed jars of sunshine from

Batgirl near the rare flowers that Abby Holland had given to her, to give them an extra boost, and they were thriving.

"I need practice," Poison Ivy said to Bumblebee. "Fighting evil beings, no problem. Rescuing citizens, no problem. Public speaking . . . scary!"

"Maybe I can help," Bumblebee offered. "You could practice interviewing me."

A look of relief washed over Ivy's face. "You would do that?" she said. "Oh, Bumblebee, that would make me so happy. Can we start tomorrow?"

CHAPTER 13

The next day, Bumblebee and Poison Ivy were all laughs and smiles when they entered Capes & Cowls. The practice interviews had gone well, and they'd made plans for more, though Ivy had pointed out, "It's so much easier interviewing a friend than someone you just met."

"Remember to breathe," Bumblebee had reminded her. Though it seemed like such an easy thing to do, one time Ivy had been so nervous she had forgotten how to inhale and exhale and had almost fallen over.

"My treat," Ivy sang as they sat at a window table. Nearby, some students from their rival school, CAD Academy, were playing checkers. Only, instead of using the checkerboard, they were throwing the pieces at each other.

"Two teas, one with extra honey for Bumblebee, please," Ivy said to Steve Trevor.

His lanky frame hunched over a bit as he reached for

the pencil that was tucked behind his ear to write the order down. Steve looked at Bumblebee. "You're not gonna want to hear this," he said, "but we're low on honey."

Bumblebee blinked in disbelief. "Low on honey? How can that be? Did someone forget to order it?"

Steve ran his hands through his thick blond hair. "Nope, we have a standing order for honey," he said, adding, "I know you always want extra on everything. But our supplier said that with the honey supply decreasing, the price has skyrocketed, and I've decided it's too pricey for us. I'm sorry, Bumblebee."

Bumblebee squelched the urge to panic. Her brains and dedication and ideas fueled her, and her super suit gave her powers, but honey sure did help, too! Didn't Beast Boy once quip, "A Bumblebee without honey is one bummed-out bee"?

"Okay," she said dejectedly, "then just tea, and how about some orange scones?"

Steve hesitated. "How about plain scones?" he asked. "Oranges . . ."

"Let me guess," Ivy said. "Oranges are getting scarce, too?"

"And strawberries, and other fresh fruits and vegetables." He shook his head. "It's the strangest thing, but some farms have them and others don't."

It was very bizarre. Bumblebee had the feeling she was going to need to look into it.

"Could it be the weather?" Bumblebee wondered out loud as she bit into her wedge-shaped scone. It had a sweet sugar glaze on it, but orange would have been nice—and to dip it in honey would have been heavenly. She noted that her Darjeeling tea tasted a bit toasty without her usual honey, but the brown sugar cubes Steve put on the table helped.

"I haven't heard of any bad weather affecting crops," Poison Ivy noted. She was trying to eat her scone with a fork and knife, and it kept crumbling.

"Hey, hey, hay is for horses!" a green horse said as it trotted to their table. Beast Boy turned back into a teen and sat down with them. "What are we talking about?" he asked. When he reached for Bumblebee's scone, she picked it up before he could get it.

"There's a shortage of honey," she said.

"And lots of fruits and veggies," Ivy added.

"Honey I can live without!" Beast Boy cried overdramatically, giving Bumblebee a wink. "But fruit and veggies I gotta have!" Then he continued in a normal voice. "Hey, BB, when are we gonna work on that tornado project?"

Bumblebee looked surprised. Since when did Beast Boy want to work on anything? "Tonight?" she said. "After dinner."

"You got it!" he said, morphing back into a horse and trotting away.

Bumblebee returned to her tea and scone. "That was weird," she noted. "I thought he was just a goof-off. He never pays attention in class."

"Give them a chance and people can surprise you," said Poison Ivy.

Later that afternoon, when Bumblebee called her parents, she asked them why it was taking so long to rebuild the house . . . and her lab.

"It's the perfect time to make some changes I've always wanted to do," Ms. Andrena-Beecher explained. "Like skylights. They'll let more sunshine in."

"How are you doing?" her father asked.

"Things are okay," Bumblebee said. Knowing how much her parents worried about her, she wasn't about to mention that her battery pack seemed to be losing more and more power each day. Recharging it seemed to be a full-time job. She was hardly flying at all, much less shrinking, and she didn't dare try to use her sonic blasters.

"Although . . . ," she said.

"Although what?" her mother quickly asked. It was amazing how tuned in to things moms were.

"Although," Bumblebee continued, "there is some sort of

shortage of honey and produce."

"I've noticed that, too," her dad said. She knew how much he liked his apple a day. "Better stock up while you can!"

Bumblebee nodded. That wasn't a bad idea, and if she was going to have Beast Boy as a study partner, she'd sure need honey to help get her through the ordeal!

That evening, before meeting up with Beast Boy, Bumblebee opened her closet door. On a shelf were jars of honey—some she had bought, some were gifts from the Honey Bees, and others were from friends and family. There was one jar that had a photo of her parents on it. They had given it to her as a joke. The label read ICE—In Case of Emergency!

In the photo, her mom and dad were making funny faces. This gave Bumblebee a tiny pang in her stomach. Unlike a lot of the other Supers, she got homesick from time to time. Bumblebee counted how many jars she had, then did the math to figure out how much she should ration. What if the honey shortage went on for weeks? Was that even possible?

She opened a jar from the Honey Bees. This one was from the group in Yunnan, China. *Just a taste,* Bumblebee thought. *Just a little.*

That night, after a moderately successful meeting with

Beast Boy, Bumblebee made sure her super suit was plugged into the charger. Feeling guilty, she glanced over at the empty jar of honey. Bumblebee hadn't meant to eat the whole thing, but . . . well, it was honey . . . and it was *soooo* delicious.

This shortage better be over soon, Bumblebee told herself. It had to be, or else at this rate, her stockpile would disappear in no time—and how would she ever get through Super Hero High without it?

CHAPTER 14

The following morning, even though Bumblebee was getting her breakfast on the run, she couldn't help but notice a few things as she made her way through the cafeteria. Cheetah was munching on seven-grain toast without jam, Hawkgirl was spooning up Wholly Oats cereal without fruit, and Starfire was eating a bran muffin—without berries. Instead of orange juice, Beast Boy guzzled chocolate milk, and Wonder Woman sipped coffee (which she immediately spat out, having never tasted coffee before).

Bumblebee stared at her own tea and realized that it contained only the teeniest, tiniest dollop of honey. *These little shortages really are getting strange,* she thought. *And the bees—what would cause them to produce less honey?* She hoped nothing was wrong with them.

Later, as Liberty Belle went on about the Natural Disaster Project, Supergirl nudged Bumblebee. "You were daydreaming," she whispered.

Supergirl was right. Bumblebee had been daydreaming, about a beautiful place with a lush garden filled with colorful flowers. Honeybees were buzzing everywhere and heading to and from their hives, which were heavy with thick golden honey.

"And because of that," Bumblebee heard Beast Boy announcing, "I predict that my partner Bumblebee and I will ace this Natural Disaster Project!"

"Wha . . . ?" she said.

"He just told the class that you two have an incredible plan to battle tornadoes," Supergirl told her.

"Is that right, Bumblebee?" Liberty Belle asked.

"Whatever he says," she answered.

Beast Boy beamed and gave her two thumbs up. "Teammates!" he said happily. "With me as the captain."

Bumblebee tried not to laugh. That would only encourage him. Plus, she didn't want to let on that she was actually starting to like being his partner. Beast Boy reminded Bumblebee of her Bee Tree Lab. To an outsider, it may have appeared to be a mess, but once you got to know how it worked, it was actually quite remarkable.

On her way to Principal Waller's office, Bumblebee decided to power up and take a short flight. It felt good to make her way down the flight lane. Students had the option of walking, running, or morphing and flying to get where they needed to go. The only rules, according to Hawkgirl, who was head hall monitor, were *"Don't* impede traffic, *keep moving*, and *be courteous* to your fellow Supers."

CRASH!

Supers were tumbling over each other before landing on their feet. "I am *sooooooo* sorry," Bumblebee said as Hawkgirl helped her up. "Are you going to write me up for an infraction?"

"Not if you have a good reason for stopping midair and then crashing down onto everyone," Hawkgirl said.

Bumblebee shook her head. "My battery," she moaned. "It just stopped. Usually I get a warning. But not this time."

"Okay," said Hawkgirl sympathetically. She adjusted her red Nth Metal belt, which held her mace. "You didn't do it on purpose. However, might I suggest you get that battery fixed?"

"I'm working on it, but—"

"Bumblebee!" Waller called out from her office. "I need you to fly this to Police Commissioner Gordon ASAP. He's teaching his forensics class, and I want him to see it before he heads back to the station."

James Gordon, the police commissioner, was also a teacher at Super Hero High. That was how his daughter, Barbara Gordon, also known as Batgirl, had learned about the school and gotten interested in it. In a short time, Batgirl had gone from Super Hero High's tech whiz, helping the students and staff with the technology issues, to a full-time student.

"I'm sorry, Principal Waller," Bumblebee said, racing into Waller's office. "I can't do that."

Waller looked up from the massive pile of papers that threatened to overtake her desk. "Excuse me? I thought I heard you say 'I can't do that.' That's not a phrase we say here at Super Hero High."

Bumblebee's heart was racing. The last person she ever wanted to disappoint was Amanda Waller. "Well," she began, "it's just that I had a crash recently, and I can't fly anymore. That is, not until I recharge my super suit. But even then, well, as you know, my lab was decimated. I was working on a new battery pack system, but now I have to start from the beginning. In the meantime, I'm dealing with a faulty battery, and I know . . . I know . . . it's a pain, and it's getting in the way of my job as office aide. And I want you to know how much I *love* this job. But if you'd rather fire me and get someone else, I totally understand."

With that, Bumblebee turned around and began to drag herself out of the office.

"STOP!" Principal Waller ordered.

"Yes?" Bumblebee said softly. She was waiting to hear that she was fired, that she had disappointed Waller, and that perhaps she shouldn't even be attending Super Hero High School.

Waller handed her an envelope. "If your batteries don't work, you can walk this, instead of fly it, to Commissioner Gordon."

"I'm not fired?" Bumblebee stammered.

The principal shook her head. "I would never discipline a student for something out of their control. But there is one thing you can do for me."

"Name it!" said Bumblebee, brightening.

"Get on the battery situation!"

"Yes, Principal Waller!" Bumblebee said, skipping out of the office as Waller tried not to crack a smile. If students saw her smiling too much, it could ruin her reputation.

"How goes your battery pack project?" Batgirl asked as she digitized the WWD, the World Weather Database—something Waller had asked her to do. Even though she was no longer the school's official tech whiz, Batgirl still got called in on special projects.

"Batteries, batteries, batteries," Bumblebee grumbled, and recounted what had happened in the hallway. "Without proper batteries, my super suit might as well be a set of pajamas. My ability to shrink and grow, my flight, my sonic blasters—I can't use anything when my batteries are dead."

Batgirl walked over. "You mind if I take a look?"

"Have at it," Bumblebee said. "The battery pack is in the back." Even though she knew she needed a solution to her problem, and quickly, Bumblebee was having trouble getting motivated. Dr. Arkham had told her that most likely, she was still devastated by the Bee Tree crash and the destruction of her family home.

"What can I do?" Bumblebee had asked him.

He had set down the book he was reading, written by himself, and said, "If someone needs help from the Supers, what do they do?"

Now Bumblebee took a deep breath. She recalled Dr. Arkham's question. "Hey, Batgirl. Um, would you mind teaming up with me to brainstorm solutions?" Bumblebee paused, then added, "I could really use some help."

Batgirl grinned. "I was hoping you'd ask! I've already written down some ideas but didn't want you to think I was being pushy!"

CHAPTER 15

Bumblebee and Batgirl stayed up late into the night, brainstorming.

"What would really be useful, instead of single-use battery packs, is one that's self-regenerating," Bumblebee told Batgirl. They were taking inventory of the Bat-tools. Everything Bumblebee could think of, and even things she couldn't imagine what they were for, were there. All were stamped with Batgirl's logo. Bumblebee reminded herself to be a little more on the ball with her own branding.

"I'd like to do some electrochemistry experiments," she went on. "And I like your idea of a mega battery source. We just have to figure out what that might be."

"Why do you keep yawning?" Beast Boy asked. They were in the library after school, and he refused to stop changing shape—and chattering. First he was a parrot, then a prairie dog, then a chimp. "Are you trying to tell me I'm boring? Because no one has ever told me that before," a chastened Beast Boy chimpanzee asked, scratching his armpit.

Bumblebee's sparkling laugh put a smile back on his face. "You're anything but boring, but please slow down! I didn't get much sleep last night," she admitted.

"Slow down?" asked Beast Boy. "I can do that for my disaster partner!"

"Can you call me something else?" Bumblebee asked the green sloth hanging upside down from the rafters. " 'Disaster partner' sounds like I'm a mess!"

Beast Boy shook his head. "Bumblebee, you're the furthest thing from a disaster!" he said sincerely.

She tried unsuccessfully to stop blushing. "Please stop slothing. We've got a lot to do."

As the two began talking tornadoes, Bumblebee was impressed by how smart Beast Boy was, though this shouldn't have been a surprise. After all, he had helped the Junior Detective Society crack lots of cases.

"Here's what I was thinking," he said, landing on two feet. Bumblebee was glad Beast Boy was back to being himself. Of all his transformations, his own basic green-teen self was her favorite. "Maybe if we understand how tornadoes begin, then we can figure out how to end them."

"Exactly my thought, too!" Bumblebee exclaimed.

As they continued exchanging ideas, all around them, teams were working on their Natural Disaster Projects. Batgirl and Barda were bent on taming storm systems. After much arguing, Cyborg and Cheetah settled on avalanches. Frost and The Flash were working on blocking blizzards. And Thunder and Lightning, who knew more about weather than anyone, were there to answer questions and assist whenever they could.

After a few hours of researching, Beast Boy suggested they take a snack break. "All this talk about tornadoes and rapidly rotating storm systems is make me dizzy," he said. To make a point, he stood up, walked in circles, and then fell on the floor.

Harley cartwheeled over. "Be careful where you fall," she said. "You don't want anyone to trip!"

Bumblebee stretched her arms. A couple of weeks ago, this would have been a good time for a honey break. But with the honey shortage, she didn't want to dip into her supply.

"What about popcorn?" Beast Boy suggested as he got up off the floor. "Or, I know!" he said, turning into an elephant. "Peanuts!"

As the two sat outside on a bench, munching on roasted peanuts, they could see Poison Ivy working in her greenhouse. Her normally happy self looked serious. "Come on," Bumblebee said to Beast Boy.

"Where to?" he asked.

"Are you all right?" Bumblebee asked Poison Ivy. The meticulously curated rows of plants seemed to go on for miles. "Do you need us to help you?"

"'Us'?" asked Beast Boy, backing away. "What's this 'us' business?"

"Sure," Poison Ivy said, looking relieved. "When Harley invited me to host *Greenhouse Hullabaloo,* I had no idea how much work it would be!"

"Your last interview, the one with the forestry agent agronomist, went well," Bumblebee told her. It was true. Ivy had forgotten how to talk only once or twice.

"Thanks!" Poison Ivy said brightly. "I still get nervous, but it's so important to feature these amazing scientists. So what's up with you, Bumblebee?" she asked as the trio began pulling weeds.

Bumblebee let out a deep sigh. "Batgirl's been letting me share the Bat-Bunker, but I don't want to overstay my welcome. It's frustrating and feels like it's taking forever to create a new battery system."

"Batteries," said Ivy. "I know lots about plants, but I'm no battery expert."

Beast Boy, who was poking around the sweet potato crop, spoke up. "I know everything about batteries," he boasted.

"Oh yeah?" said Bumblebee. "Tell us."

Beast Boy stood up and cleared his throat. "Batteries are things we use to juice up our computers and stuff!"

"Well . . . yes, but how do they work?" Bumblebee said, locking eyes with Ivy. The two smiled at each other.

"Um, you know," said Beast Boy.

"I do," said Bumblebee. "The most common battery cell has three parts: an anode, which is a negative charge; a cathode, which is a positive charge; and, of course, as everyone knows, the third is an electrolyte, the chemical medium that facilitates the flow of electrical charge between the other two. When something is connected to the battery, the chemical reactions occur on the electrodes to create a flow of electrical energy."

Beast Boy nodded slowly and turned to Poison Ivy. "Hmmm," he said, stroking his chin. "I believe she's right. Yep. That's what I was going to say."

CHAPTER 16

It was so much easier to address her battery problem now that she had Batgirl to bounce ideas off of. "It seems so old-school, the way batteries are made," Bumblebee lamented. "Plus, they're really expensive, especially for something as complicated as my super suit."

"Ooomph!" Batgirl fell over and held up the spiky weed that she had been trying to excise from the ground. "Got it!" she yelled triumphantly as Harley shot video for the next *Greenhouse Hullabaloo*—a "sneak-peek behind-the-scenes spectacular on the world's largest plant nursery."

The greenhouse was laid out like a United Nations of plants. Flora from various countries were all growing side by side, divided only by narrow dirt walkways. There were farmlands, a cactus garden, a tropical paradise, and more. And all of it was overseen by Poison Ivy.

Luckily, once word got out, lots of Supers volunteered to help, even teaming up their complementary powers. Supergirl was surrounded by cacti, using her heat vision to create the dry air of a desert environment around them, while El Diablo used his fire power to regulate the temperature of tropical microenvironments. Meanwhile, Katana was using swords, one in each hand, to cut back the overgrowth and trim trees, and Catwoman was trying to coax the corpse flower, the stinkiest plant in the world, to bloom.

As Batgirl lay on her back, she looked up through the glass ceiling. "Hey, that one looks like a tree," she said, pointing to a cloud.

Bumblebee lay down beside her. "It reminds me of the Bee Tree," she noted. "And look, there's a dragon!"

"I hope it's not Dragon King," Katana said as she joined them. "That would be bad news!" She singled out a cloud in the distance. "That one looks like a castle."

"And there's the queen!" exclaimed Bumblebee as she watched the clouds float by on a sea of blue sky. *A queen and a castle,* she mused. *What a lovely thought.*

"Okay," Bumblebee declared. "I'm ready!"

She was back in the Bat-Bunker with Batgirl. The two had found a temporary solution to her battery pack problem. After taking several batteries, welding them together, and then supercharging them, they were finally able to apply them to the super suit.

"It's heavy, but I can handle it," Bumblebee assured Batgirl. "Give me a countdown!"

"Three . . . two . . . one . . . blastoff!" Batgirl yelled.

A brilliant smile lit up on Bumblebee's face as she began to attain liftoff. As she flew in tight circles around the Bat-Bunker, Bumblebee felt light and happy, a feeling she hadn't had since the Bee Tree crashed into her house.

"Okay," she told Batgirl. "I'm going to do it!"

"You sure?" Batgirl asked.

"Better now, under test conditions, than out in the open," Bumblebee said.

Batgirl nodded. "Copy that," she said. "I'll count you down again. Three . . . two . . . one . . . NOW!"

In a split second, Bumblebee went from big to bee-sized. Her heart raced with happiness as she swooped around the room, doing aerial somersaults and dips and dives. "Wheeeeee!" she shouted over Batgirl's cheers. But suddenly she felt a jolt. "Uh-oh" was the last thing she said before the crash. "Ouch! Ouch! Ouch! And did I say 'ouch'?"

Batgirl was by her side. "What happened?" she asked.

"My suit misfired," Bumblebee told her. "I wasn't in control when I started to grow big again, and it threw me off balance so much that I was forced to crash-land."

"Luckily, we weren't outside, over a ravine, or in battle," Batgirl noted.

Bumblebee nodded. "I am so sorry," she said. She got up off Batgirl's table, which was now flattened. Tools were scattered everywhere. Bumblebee felt awful. Not just sore from the fall, but awful in the pit of her stomach, and in her head, and in her heart. As she started to gather the tools off the floor, she didn't feel much like a super hero.

PART
TWO

CHAPTER 17

"The good news is that when the house is done, you'll have a brand-new tech lab!" Ms. Andrena-Beecher said brightly.

"Thanks, Mom," said Bumblebee. "But I think maybe I ought to also be thinking about creating a lab here at Super Hero High. Batgirl's been letting me use her Bat-Bunker, and I realize how convenient it is to have one where I live."

"Oh, okay," her mother said softly. "Well, that does make sense. But we're rebuilding your room for when you come home. You will still come home for Sunday suppers, right? And weekends now and then, like before?"

Bumblebee could hear the worry in her mom's voice. Sometimes Bumblebee was so busy talking about all the amazing, fun, and scary things that happened at school, she forgot that her parents were always thinking about her. Bumblebee made a mental note to call them more often. After all, she was their only child.

"Of course, Mom," Bumblebee reassured her. "I will always come home, I promise! How else will I get in my Mom and Dad fix?"

Ms. Andrena-Beecher's laugh sounded like crystal bells ringing. "You have always been good at sweet-talking us, Bumblebee," she said.

Bumblebee could hear her father in the background, saying, "Is that our daughter? Tell her that I'm still taking photos. Just because my photo studio is gone doesn't mean I have to stop."

"Bumblebee," her mother began, "your father said that he's still taking photos—"

"I know, Mom," she said. "I could hear him."

Bumblebee missed her parents. Sometimes they could drive her crazy, but then, most of her friends said the same thing about their parents. Just then, what sounded like the rat-tat-tat of explosives carried over the phone. Bumblebee startled.

"Whoops! Excuse me, honey," said her mother. "That's just me sneezing. Allergies. The pollen is unseasonably strong today!"

Bumblebee let go a sigh of relief. "I'm glad it was just a sneeze," she said. "For a moment, I thought it was something worse."

As Bumblebee walked through Centennial Park to meet Beast Boy, the plants looked like they were wilting. She had been doing a lot of walking lately, to conserve her batteries. For the first time, Bumblebee had even asked to sit out and observe during Red Tornado's Flight Training class.

The sound of sneezes filled the park. Everywhere they went, Bumblebee and Beast Boy observed people sneezing and dabbing their eyes with tissues. As she neared a familiar cluster of evergreen trees, Bumblebee slowed. She loved greeting the honeybees who inhabited several hives nestled in the tall branches. Usually there were bees buzzing around, and Bumblebee would get bee-sized and fly along with them. Though she couldn't speak their language, they seemed to be fond of her, and she certainly was a fan of theirs.

The hives were unusually quiet. In the distance, Bumblebee could hear sneezes, but what she couldn't hear was the low, sweet buzz of the bees.

"Hello?" she called up. "It's me, Bumblebee!"

She always called ahead before visiting. It was never a good idea to disturb a hive. The bees might think you were trying to invade and would attack to defend their queen.

"Hello?" Bumblebee called again.

There was no answer, no group of bees to greet her. Instead, strangely, there was silence.

"Maybe you offended them and they don't want to see

you," Beast Boy said as he walked up to her. "Or maybe they're on a field trip. Remember when we all went to the Great Pyramid of Giza yesterday afternoon? Or maybe they're on vacation."

Bumblebee shook her head. "That's not how bees work," she said.

"Bees work?" asked Beast Boy. "I thought they just buzzed around sniffing the flowers." He morphed into an energetic hummingbird and flew away but then came back a few minutes later. "Couldn't find any flowers," he said, turning back into a teen.

"Bees work really, really hard," Bumblebee explained. As they headed to the Metropolis Library, Beast Boy kept waving to everyone he knew, or didn't know but wanted to know—which was everyone.

"Bees fly around from flower to flower," Bumblebee continued, "sipping the sweet nectar while collecting tiny grains of pollen. When they have as much as they can carry, they head back to their hives, where it's turned into honey." She paused, thinking of honey and how she was now down to three jars. And they weren't even big jars.

"Hives? I got hives once," Beast Boy said, his eyes lighting up at the memory of it. "Big bumps all over my body. It was awful and awesome at the same time. So I turned into an alligator until they were gone. Wanna see a photo?"

Bumblebee shook her head. "No, thank you. These hives are where bees live. Here they work together, and every bee has a job to do, starting with the queen, who lays the eggs."

"How many queens are there?" Beast Boy asked. He sneezed so loud that Rainbow the cat jumped out of Scooter's arms and up a tree.

"Just one per hive," Bumblebee told him. "Everyone else works for her." She brushed a light dusting of yellow off her super suit. *What is this?*

CHAPTER 18

The pollen started drifting down so slowly that hardly anyone noticed at first. It was the sneezing that caused the commotion.

"The weather is unusually warm," noted Mr. Fox as he pulled handkerchief after handkerchief out of his pocket like a magician and sneezed into them. "I wonder if this has anything to do with it. Poison Ivy, any idea where all this pollen is coming from? *Achoooo!*"

"I'm already on it!" she declared. "Watch Harley's *Greenhouse Hullabaloo* tonight."

Greenhouse Hullabaloo was amassing a huge audience and was one of Harley's most popular shows. Most viewers tuned in to see what amazing, exotic, and wondrous plants Ivy would feature, like . . . a talking flower! Plants that turned themselves into famous sculptures! A tiny cactus that could hold hundreds of gallons of water! But there was an enthusiastic portion of the audience who watched specifically to cheer on Poison Ivy. Her flubs and flusters were winning her a new legion of fans.

That night, several Supers gathered in Wonder Woman's room to watch the show.

"Dr. Akita-Janowitz," Ivy was asking a jaunty-looking botanist whose vest pockets were overflowing with gardening tools, serious scientific implements, and lollipops, "what is your took—er, talk—er, take—take on the pollen saturation—er, situation?"

"Speak up, dear," Dr. Akita-Janowitz chided her host. "I can't hear you."

Ivy blushed and blinked at the camera apologetically. "Sorry, sorry," she said, then took a deep breath. "WHAT IS YOUR TAKE ON THE POLLEN SITUATION??!!!!"

The botanist and the viewers covered their ears. "No need to shout, Ms. Ivy." Dr. Akita-Janowitz lowered her voice. "It's not good for the more delicate plants."

She motioned to the ghost orchids and chocolate cosmos that were still trembling. When Ivy knelt and cradled the fragile flowers in her hands, you could practically hear the audience exhale a group "Ooooooh."

"I'm sorry, Casper. So sorry, Luminus," Ivy said, looking so concerned that some viewers got weepy.

As the interview went on, Dr. Akita-Janowitz admitted that even she, one of the top botanists in the world, was at a loss to identify the source of the pollen that was causing so many people's sinuses to go haywire. At the end of the show, Poison Ivy thanked her distinguished guest and then, blushing, said, "So, um, from Harley's Purple House, er, Greenhouse Hubba, Hubba, um, Hulla, Hello . . ."

Dr. Akita-Janowitz stuck her head into the frame and said helpfully, "*Greenhouse Hullabaloo,* starring everyone's favorite plant pal, Poison Ivy!"

"And Casper and Quuminus, or is it Jasper and Luminus?" Ivy said as she nervously twisted her long red braid.

Bumblebee shook her head. "I told Ivy that there are just way too many plants there for her to name all of them."

Wonder Woman, who was munching on popcorn sprinkled with shredded Parmesan cheese, nodded. Through a mouthful, she said, "Anyone else notice that ever since the show, Ivy's been distracted?"

"It's no wonder," Bumblebee said. "She's putting all her time into the greenhouse."

"Well, it *is* the largest in the world," Big Barda pointed out. She looked at Wonder Woman's bowl of popcorn. "You gonna finish that?"

"Yes," said Wonder Woman, defensively pulling her bowl closer to her chest.

"I'm here with more!" Supergirl announced as she passed out more popcorn. "I heard that Ivy was so busy with the greenhouse that she forgot a major assignment in Liberty Belle's class."

Eyes widened. The only times Waller allowed students to make up an assignment were when they were needed in a battle, citizens had to be saved, a crime had to be thwarted, or they had a note from the school nurse or their parents.

"Someone should tell her to ask more people to help with the greenhouse," Bumblebee declared. "Us Supers helping is not enough. Plus, we all have school, just like Poison Ivy."

"School, schmool," Harley quipped as she tossed three empty popcorn bowls in the air. "What's a little multitasking, anyway?"

"Not everyone is as good at juggling as you are," noted Barda as she watched Harley add a bowling ball to the popcorn bowls and keep them all in the air at once.

"Well," said Harley, "that's true. I guess there's money in the show budget for her to hire an assistant."

"It's settled, then!" Wonder Woman said. "Who will tell Poison Ivy?"

"How's about her?" Harley said, pointing to Bumblebee. "It was her idea!"

"What are they saying?" Big Barda asked Supergirl.

"I don't know," Supergirl said. They were looking where Ivy and Bumblebee stood facing each other some distance away in the orchid section of the greenhouse.

"Well, you have superhearing. You can just tune in," Barda insisted.

"It's only for emergencies, to save lives, and when there is general danger and mayhem," Supergirl explained.

Barda faced Miss Martian. "You can read minds," she said to the shy alien from Mars. "What are they thinking?"

Miss Martian shifted uncomfortably. "I can't tell you that," she said softly.

"Sure you can," Barda insisted good-naturedly.

"I only use my power for—" Miss Martian began.

"I know, I know," Barda said. "It's only for emergencies, to save lives, and when there is general danger and mayhem."

Bumblebee and Ivy had their heads together. Both looked serious. First Bumblebee would talk and Poison Ivy would nod. Then Poison Ivy would talk and Bumblebee would nod. Then both were nodding.

"I can't stand this!" Big Barda said. She ran over to the two of them and asked, "What are you saying?"

Bumblebee looked at Ivy. "Are you going to tell her, or shall I do it?"

Poison Ivy let go of a sigh. "I will," she said. "Despite my reservations, I'm going to hire someone to help me take care of the greenhouse. The ad will go out tomorrow."

"Look happy about it," Bumblebee encouraged her friend. "None of us likes asking for help, but this will make your life easier, and that way you can focus on what we're all here for—to prepare to be the best super heroes we can be!"

Reluctantly, Ivy nodded. "Yes," she said. "But what if no one applies?"

CHAPTER 19

"I'm glad Ivy is taking out that ad," Batgirl was saying to Bumblebee. They were in the Bat-Bunker. "She's so overworked, but despite what she thinks, she can't do everything by herself."

"Don't I know it!" Bumblebee said. What was it that made the Supers think they could do it all? "We're trained to help others. But we're not so good about asking others for help."

Batgirl nodded. She picked up two pairs of laser-shield goggles and handed one to Bumblebee. "Safety first!" Both slipped them on. Then Bumblebee pressed the glowing yellow button.

Instantly, an alarm sounded. Red lights flashed as the two Supers stared at an object the size of a bowling ball. It rested on a stand inside the triple-glass enclosure that Bumblebee had fabricated using ultra-aerodynamic levitation to form the world's highest and strongest protective barrier. Lasers spun before they all focused and hit the object. It lit up, then began to sizzle, until—BOOM! And then the room went dark.

Batgirl took off her goggles and said dejectedly, "Lights, on." The room lit up.

Bumblebee was staring at what was left of the burnt object. Smoke billowed from it. "So much for that battery," she said. Using Bumblebee's engineering calculations and Batgirl's computer wizardry, they had been trying various batteries for her super suit. But none had worked the way Bumblebee needed it to.

There was a knock on the door. "Hello," a voice said outside the Bat-Bunker. "Everything all right in there?"

Batgirl looked at the security monitor and buzzed Poison Ivy in.

"Good news!" Ivy announced. Her face was flushed with excitement. "I've finally narrowed down the search for an assistant! But I could really use your help testing the finalists tomorrow."

Hundreds of people had applied to work with Ivy, but now there were only three: Petey Bogg, Jason Woodrue, and Karena Tisk. Each was given a written test, a plant problem, and a worst-case scenario.

The written test consisted of identifying some of the rarer

and more exotic plants, and all three scored well. The plant problem proved more challenging.

Ivy had set up an obstacle course for the applicants. With Batgirl manning the timers, they each were challenged with watering, feeding, and caring for dozens of plants from different parts of the world. Petey Bogg slipped up and spread fertilizer over the cactus garden, but Jason Woodrue and Karena Tisk each managed to weave through the obstacle course, picking just-ripened fruits and pulling weeds, without any problems. However, when they were getting ready for the worst-case scenario, a real worst-case scenario began to materialize.

Poison Ivy wanted to see how they would respond when a plant was in danger of being overwatered. Bumblebee had just created an indoor arch-gravity dam and tributaries to create a flood, when what sounded like an engine humming got louder and louder. She checked the dam, but it wasn't coming from there. That was when Petey Bogg pointed up. "Bug! Big bug comin' at us!" he yelled, and ran out of the greenhouse.

Sure enough, a man-sized bug was perched on the glass roof. He smiled menacingly and waved at Poison Ivy, Batgirl, and Bumblebee.

"Firefly!" Poison Ivy gasped. "He hates beautiful gardens and is always trying to burn them down."

"I'll handle this," Bumblebee said, pressing her power button. Nothing happened. The last five times they had tested the battery pack in the Bat-Bunker, it had worked beautifully. She pressed the button again. Nothing.

Meanwhile, Firefly had used his fusion laser to cut through the glass and was flapping his metallic wings as he flew around the greenhouse.

"HELP!" yelled Karena Tisk when she saw him. She was in such a panic she ran right into the rare, sticky, and stinky Koloff tree and got stuck. "I'm scared of bugs," she wailed. "Get me out of here!"

Keeping her eyes on Firefly, Batgirl reached for her Batarang. "I got this," she said, sprinting toward him.

"Right behind you," said Poison Ivy as they raced toward Firefly.

"Me too?" said Bumblebee. As she ran behind her friends, Bumblebee was flooded with memories of little Karen Andrena-Beecher running around her backyard, pretending to be a super hero.

Just then, Firefly used an energy weapon to release a stream of fire and began torching the greenhouse. Batgirl flung her Batarang, knocking him over, and Poison Ivy summoned the kudzu plants from the Southeast Asia garden to envelop him.

Bumblebee charged over to the fire. She was hoping to

activate the sprinkler system when she felt the spray of a large amount of water rushing by her and putting the fire out. Jason Woodrue, knee-deep in the flood, was smiling.

"I merely opened the dam," he said, looking proud of himself. "All in the line of duty."

CHAPTER 20

For days, Poison Ivy had been gushing about how fantastic her assistant, Jason Woodrue, was with the plants. Her friends had to admit that the foliage looked absolutely lush. Jason's quick thinking had saved the greenhouse—and earned him a job. At last, Poison Ivy was back to her happy self, with great grades and enough time to spend with her friends. Everyone was in a good mood, especially since the pollen that had been making everyone sneeze disappeared as mysteriously as it had first appeared.

"It's weird," Bumblebee noted.

"It's fine by me," Barda said.

"But why?" Bumblebee asked. "Pollen. No pollen. Sneezing. No sneezing."

"Probably just a fluke of the weather?" Barda ventured. "Or maybe our natural disaster rainstorms washed the pollen away," she said, though Bumblebee didn't look convinced.

"There they are!" Supergirl said, using her super-vision

to see past the jungle, the subtropical gardens, and the court of palms.

Bumblebee squinted. She could see a tall, skinny man in the distance—or was that a tree? As her friends rushed over, Bumblebee hurried along, aware that without batteries fueling her power pack, she couldn't do nearly as much as the others.

"For those of you who haven't met him yet, this is Jason Woodrue," Ivy said proudly. "Jason, this is everyone!"

Jason put down the potted plumeriasian lavender he had been tending to. "It's a ruba hybrid, but I'm sure you all already know that," he said. His diction was clear and crisp, and his manners were impeccable.

"Um, I didn't know that," Ivy admitted.

Jason shook his head sadly and adjusted his round wire-rimmed glasses. "Well, you will," he assured her. "Now that I'm here, this greenhouse will be in tip-top shape, I can assure you of that. It won't be the shambles it was before." Poison Ivy seemed to shrink a bit, but Jason didn't notice. "Does anyone have any questions?" he said. "I know all the answers."

"Do you always dress like that?" Wonder Woman asked, pointing to his suit.

"Yes, Jason Woodrue does," he said, referring to himself. He was nattily attired in a tailored dark green tweed three-piece suit. The handkerchief in his pocket was made of blue silk, and his crisp pink shirt was complemented by a skinny tie the color of his light green eyes. "Jason feels that it is imperative to always look one's best."

He glanced at Ivy, who self-consciously pushed some of her flowing red hair out of her face. Supergirl bent down to tie her shoes, and Bumblebee brushed some cracker crumbs off her super suit. It had been days since she had had even a smidgen of honey. She had taken to putting peanut butter on everything, but it wasn't the same.

"Now, I have a question," Jason said, looking around.

"I thought you had all the answers," said Bumblebee.

He ignored her and asked, "When does Harley Quinn show up? When is Jason Woodrue going to make his debut on *Greenhouse Hullabaloo*?"

Later that day, Bumblebee asked Poison Ivy, "How's Jason working out?" They were walking to Liberty Belle's class. Both ducked just in time to avoid being hit by Beast Boy flying low as a spotted owl.

"Great," Ivy said. "Jason knows everything about plants. He used to be a botany professor!"

"I think he's a snob," said Barda. "Oops! Did I say that?"

"He's just extremely confident," Ivy said, defending her assistant. "Hey, who's going to watch the show tonight? Now that the pollen problem is gone, I'll be doing a segment about how talking to your plants makes them, and you, happy!"

Bumblebee tried not to laugh while watching *Greenhouse Hullabaloo.* Jason Woodrue managed to insert himself in every scene, and was not very subtle about it.

"When your plants seem sad, you can tell them—" Poison Ivy was saying.

"You can tell them Jason Woodrue says be happy!" he said, smiling at the camera.

As the show continued, Beast Boy knocked on Wonder Woman's dorm door. "Hey, Bumblebee," he called, "thought I'd find you here. I have an awesome surprise for you!"

"What?" she asked, not taking her eyes off the screen.

"Oh, just some . . . HONEY!" Beast Boy said, grinning.

Bumblebee turned away from the monitor, where Ivy was strolling through a section of the greenhouse. Jason was following so close they kept bumping into each other while he waved to the camera.

Beast Boy handed Bumblebee a glass jar. "I know you've been kinda blue without your honey supply," he said. "So I made this!"

"You *made* this yourself?" Bumblebee asked. She was touched that he would do that.

"Yep! Try it. It tastes *exactly* like honey." Beast Boy looked like he would burst with pride.

Bumblebee opened the jar and dipped her finger into the golden brown concoction. It felt like honey. It tasted like . . .

Beast Boy watched intently. "Well? Well?" he asked. "What did I tell you? Exactly like honey, right?"

Bumblebee pursed her lips and nodded. "Mmmmmm," she said. "Mmmmmmmm."

"You're welcome," Beast Boy said proudly. He turned into a peacock and unfolded a fan of breathtaking emerald-green tail feathers as he strutted out of the room.

"Does it really taste just like honey?" Batgirl asked.

Bumblebee waited until she was sure Beast Boy was gone and then gasped, "Water! I need water!" as she tried to wipe the fake honey off her tongue.

CHAPTER 21

"**A**nd because of that, we must make a great impression on our guests!" Principal Waller boomed from the stage. Though the auditorium was large, no microphone was necessary. Behind her, teachers sat in thronelike chairs. Bumblebee looked at Batgirl's father, Police Commissioner Gordon, who taught the forensics class. How cool was it that Batgirl got to see her dad all the time? Bumblebee made a mental note to call her parents.

Waller continued, "Remember when you were not yet students here and you toured Super Hero High?"

Everyone nodded. They did remember. For most of the Supers, it had been their goal since childhood to attend this prestigious institution of learning for super heroes. When Wonder Woman was homeschooled on Paradise Island, she watched and rewatched the recruitment video hundreds of times. For Supergirl, it was her cousin Superman who had suggested she enroll in Super Hero High to learn how to control her powers. And for Katana, upholding the legacy of Samurai warrior super heroes had brought her here.

Bumblebee leaned forward, soaking up every word Waller said. As a child, she had read all the super-hero fan magazines, poring over them so many times that the pages fell apart. Most of her favorite super heroes had gone to Super Hero High, and yes, even a few super-villains. Bumblebee had just created her super suit and was working on perfecting her shrinking when she heard about Super Hero High Visit Day. She begged her parents to take her. When they finally agreed, she was so excited she couldn't sleep the night before—or the night after.

Meeting the legendary principal Amanda Waller and the super-hero students was a wish come true. Young Bumblebee had wondered if she dared to dream to be among their ranks someday.

"Each of you will be given an assignment," Waller was saying as she paced the stage. Several students were taking notes. Cheetah and Frost were trading secrets. The Flash and Cyborg were playfully shoving each other while Hawkgirl, who was sitting between them, tried to ignore them.

Bumblebee focused on the principal. "Some of you will be tour guides; others will help run seminars. There will be a special program for students considering transferring, and we will also have a program for parents, who always have a lot of questions."

Bumblebee had to laugh at that. She remembered that her mom and dad had each had a long list of concerns they needed addressed before they allowed her to attend.

"*Achoo!*" When Police Commissioner Gordon sneezed, Waller shot him a cool look. "Excuse me," he mumbled.

She had begun to speak again when Liberty Belle emitted a series of surprisingly loud sneezes, followed by Coach Wildcat sneezing so violently the room shook. Waller's steely look caused Crazy Quilt to freeze mid-sneeze. Several students started to snicker. Especially when Mr. Fox started pulling out his handkerchiefs with each oncoming sneeze. Soon the entire auditorium erupted in sneezes.

"Enough!" Principal Waller demanded. Then a strange look came over her face. Her nose began to twitch, and the harder she tried to hold it back, the more rigid her already-ramrod-straight posture became.

No one in the auditorium dared to breathe. But when Waller let out a surprisingly dainty sneeze, it was as if everyone was given permission to join in. Soon the room sounded like an echo chamber of sneezes.

"The pollen must be back!" Bumblebee said to Ivy. "*Achoo!*"

Poison Ivy covered her mouth, then let out a series of sneezes. "*Achoo!* That's for sure," she said. "*Achoo! Achoo! Achoo!*"

Just then, the alarm sounded. Bumblebee looked up

onstage. Principal Waller nodded to her. "Save the Day drill! Save the Day drill!" Bumblebee shouted. As Waller's trusted assistant, it was her job to inform the student body of all events, warn them of impending doom, and alert them to Save the Day drills, as well as the real thing.

Waller looked at her watch. "Let's give the teachers a thirty-minute head start for this drill, and then . . . Supers, go Save the Day!"

As Bumblebee and Beast Boy headed out, they were joined by Batgirl. In sets of three, the Supers were charged with thwarting a natural disaster that the teachers had created. Only, this wasn't on paper or in the classroom. This time, teachers and staff had placed themselves in actual perilous conditions. It was up to the Supers to use what they had been studying to test their skills and save them.

Past drills had had teachers in out-of-control vehicles, including cars, trains, rockets, and hover boats. Another had put them in the path of stampeding animals. And yet another had placed them in a forest surrounded by poisonous talking plants and mutant aliens.

"A tornado is heading straight toward Coach Wildcat!" Beast Boy exclaimed when he read their assignment. "We got this, right, Bumblebee?"

"Right!" she said happily. "We've been working on tornadoes," she explained to Batgirl.

"Well, that makes me lucky to be on your team," Batgirl said. "What are we waiting for? There's a Wildcat to be rescued!"

CHAPTER 22

Cyborg, Star Sapphire, and Frost were off to the Swiss Alps to rescue Parasite from an avalanche. The Flash, Cheetah, and Katana were already at Red Rock in Arizona, where Liberty Belle was hiking in the middle of an earthquake. And Wonder Woman, Supergirl, and Hawkgirl were flying faster than the speed of sound to get to Red Tornado, who was circling the globe and about to be hit by a meteor shower.

"According to my coordinates, Coach Wildcat should be in that barn over there," Batgirl said to Beast Boy and Bumblebee.

The three had flown to Gowin Town, Ohio, Batgirl using her jetpack, Beast Boy as an eagle, and Bumblebee with her super suit. She knew it was a risk to use her batteries, given the failure in the greenhouse. But Bumblebee had never missed a Save the Day drill, and she wasn't about to start now. However, once in flight, she noticed that her wings were causing a drag and that she didn't have the power to fly as fast as usual.

"Hurry!" Beast Boy kept yelling as they made their way over big cities and small towns, mountains and meadows.

"I'm trying," Bumblebee shouted back. She hated that she was slowing the team down.

The barn was in the middle of an apple orchard. As the Supers neared, the sky darkened. "Looks like it's going to be six or seven on my tornado Bat-scale," Batgirl said, adjusting her weather scanner as the three heroes stood on a hill overlooking the old building.

"What's that?" asked Bumblebee.

"It's my tornado intensity scale from zero to ten, with ten being the most violent," Batgirl explained. "My electronics measure the velocity of the winds, run it though a database of past tornadoes with similar numbers, then calculate the unique characteristics of the tornado at hand to come up with a number."

"Um, that's what I thought," said Beast Boy. "Hey! Tornadoes are also called twisters. And the twist is a dance! Who wants to do the twist with me?"

As he danced, Bumblebee and Batgirl formulated a plan. "We'll evacuate Wildcat," Batgirl began.

"The tornado is coming in fast from the west," Bumblebee noted. "It's zigzagging, but if we approach the barn from the east, we may be able to avoid the worst of it."

"You on board?" Batgirl asked Beast Boy.

"I'm on board," Beast Boy quipped, pretending to surf. "Let's Save the Day!"

When the trio headed toward their P.E. teacher, the dark sky began to close in around them. Soon the trees were swaying, branches were whipping around, and apples were flying like projectiles, pelting the Supers.

"Hello?" Coach Wildcat called out. "I hope I'm not interrupting anything, but is someone going to help me or what?!"

Just then, Bumblebee froze as a mammoth rumbling choked the air. The gray tornado coming toward them was gaining speed . . . and headed directly for the barn. With quick calculations, she knew they had less than three minutes if they were to rescue Wildcat.

"Inside!" shouted Bumblebee. "NOW!"

The barn was dark and its walls were quaking. "You're late," a gravelly voice growled.

"We're getting you out of here, sir," said Bumblebee as she looked for an easy escape. The barn door on the far side was bolted shut. She tried to pry it open, but without the enhanced strength from her super suit, she wasn't strong enough.

The sound of apples pelting the barn was relentless. Batgirl turned on her Bat-light. Coach Wildcat was sitting on a bale of hay, frowning.

"Let's get this show on the road!" Beast Boy said. "Since that tornado looks like an elephant's trunk, I can look like an elephant, too!"

"Stop goofing off," Bumblebee chided him. "This is serious."

"We need to get going fast," Batgirl yelled. "Come on, Coach, follow us!"

"Wait!" shouted Bumblebee. The tornado sounded like a train barreling down on them. She covered her ears.

Suddenly, the roof of the barn flew off. "Take cover!" screamed Bumblebee. "Beast Boy, stay as an elephant and lean up against that combine harvester."

The giant farm harvester looked like it weighed thousands of pounds—enough to withstand a tornado if it wasn't a direct hit, Bumblebee deduced. She joined Batgirl and Wildcat and got between the machine and the elephant as the walls began to shake and the ground beneath them buckled. With a huge whoosh, the barn boards began to splinter and then fly away as Beast Boy's elephant stood strong and the harvester refused to budge.

All at once, there was an eerie silence. Bumblebee looked

up to find the tornado passing directly overhead. They were now inside a smooth funnel of clouds, with smaller twisters above that twirled and swirled like graceful dancers before breaking free. A blue light lit up the interior of the funnel, and then BOOM! The sun was shining and the sky was blue.

Beast Boy turned back into a green teen. "Thanks," Batgirl told him as she stepped over a sea of crushed apples that littered the ground.

"Thank that harvester. If I didn't have that to lean on, you'd all be as smooshed as those apples. Applesauce, anyone?" Beast Boy quipped.

"Be careful where you step," Bumblebee warned Wildcat.

"Terrible, terrible," he muttered as he stomped away. "You three were late!"

Batgirl and Bumblebee looked at each other, troubled. Beast Boy was humming and strolling along. Not much could faze him. That was when Bumblebee tuned in to a sound she hadn't heard for a while: bees! There were bees in the area! And if there were bees, there must be beehives! And if there were beehives, there must be honey!

"Let's follow the sound of the bees," she cried happily.

"Let's go back to Super Hero High," growled the coach. "I have to write up a report on how the three of you did." He shook his head. "Not good, not good."

"We should do what Coach says," Batgirl cautioned.

Bumblebee nodded. Perhaps it was enough knowing the

bees were there. But just as she was about to head back to school, she noticed that Coach Wildcat had disappeared.

All three looked around for him. "Coach, where are you?" Bumblebee called out. Was this another part of the Save the Day drill?

Beast Boy tapped her on the shoulder and pointed.

"Coach, what are you doing up in the tree?" Bumblebee asked. She shaded her eyes from the sun.

"I didn't have a choice," he said. "They chased me up here! Now get me down. These bees are angry and about to start stinging!"

CHAPTER 23

While the team of Wonder Woman, Supergirl, and Hawkgirl were lauded for a spectacular Save the Day drill rescue of Red Tornado—and for redirecting the meteors that had threatened to pelt him and the Earth—others weren't as lucky. Batgirl, Bumblebee, and Beast Boy were assigned to write a paper about the tornado rescue, analyzing what had gone wrong and including a plan on how to respond more quickly should that natural disaster happen again.

Beast Boy was munching on a veggie submarine sandwich. "Hey! You two are much better writers than me, so how about I sit back and let you do your thing," he said between bites. "Then I'll sweep in at the end to look it over, and we can all sign the paper."

Bumblebee tried to ignore him. But as she watched him eating, she wished she had some bread and honey. Or tea and honey. Or anything and honey! One way or another, she was going to have to get to the bottom of the bee problem, but right now, the sound of everyone sneezing was making it hard to focus, especially when someone like Supergirl sneezed and blew all the library books off the shelves. Or when Frost sneezed and froze Miss Martian, who had to be thawed out by El Diablo, who had to be monitored by Hawkgirl, lest he sneeze while sending out flames and accidentally light her on fire.

"You know," mused Bumblebee, "we didn't sneeze at all when we were rescuing Coach Wildcat."

"That's true," Batgirl said. "And none of the others mentioned sneezing during their Save the Day drills."

"There was no sneezing in the Alps or in the Arizona desert, and others reported that no one sneezed in outer space, Finland, or Bora Bora," Bumblebee concurred. "It seems like it's isolated in and around Super Hero High and a few other areas."

"It's a totally regional thing," Beast Boy noted. He took a bag of chips out of his backpack and began munching and sneezing, accidentally spewing potato chips on the girls.

"Ewww!" said Batgirl, jumping up and wiping off her Batsuit.

"What she said!" Bumblebee cried. "Watch where you spew." When she brushed some chips off her super suit, she noticed a dusting of yellow pollen again. Bumblebee stared at it on her fingertips, then said, "Hey, let's ask Ivy to join us in Mr. Fox's science lab. I want to determine whether this pollen is coincidence . . . or conspiracy."

Poison Ivy looked up from the petri dish she was studying under the microscope. "Dr. Akita-Janowitz couldn't identify this pollen because it's man-made," she concluded. "It causes sneezing, and drowsiness if delivered in mega mega doses."

"Is it deadly?" Bumblebee was quick to ask. Since she had been using Mr. Fox's lab so often lately, he had allowed her to set up some personal research space in the corner of the room.

Ivy shook her head. "It's not lethal. The sleep-inducing potential is so minimal it would only work on a tiny creature. But why anyone would create something like that is a mystery."

The Supers had lots of questions but not a whole lot of answers, and there wasn't time to get into it anyway.

"Since no lives are in danger, you can investigate after Super Hero High Visitor Day," Waller said. "We've dealt with mutant armies, evil criminals, and mountains imploding, so what harm is a little sneezing? For now, I want any of your spare time to be focused on our upcoming event."

That meant that the massive sculpture Katana was carving of Onna-bugeisha, her super-hero Samurai grandmother, would be put on hold. And so would the new show Harley was creating, *Harley's Pampered Pets*, featuring the world's richest animals.

As the principal's key aide, Bumblebee had her hands full. With all the errands she had to run, it sure would have been easier to fly around the school, but her battery pack was holding even less of a charge than before. Sure, there were times when Bumblebee could fly for a full twenty minutes, but other times she could only go for three and then needed to recharge.

Bumblebee tried to hide how worried she was. This wasn't the first time she'd had problems with her super suit. There was that time when she was bee-sized and didn't have enough battery power to make herself transform back to full-sized. It was so scary, and it wasn't until—

"Tissues?" Waller asked.

"What? Oh, yes," Bumblebee said. She was working extra hard and trying to make herself indispensable to Waller. The last thing she wanted was for the principal to think she wasn't super-hero material. "Yes, tissues are under control," Bumblebee assured her. "And if we run out, I know where there's a stockpile." She recalled Dr. Arkham's supply.

Bumblebee had managed to secure several truckloads of tissues and assigned Supers to hand them out the second a visitor's nose began to twitch. Good thing, because amid the sneezes, Super Hero High Visitor Day soon arrived and guests started to stream in.

It seemed like everyone's eyes were watering, and the sneezing was echoing between the buildings and ricocheting down the hallways of the school. Even Amanda Waller couldn't help but let out a sneeze or two. However, there was one visitor who didn't appear affected.

Bumblebee couldn't help but stare. The woman looked like a glamorous old-time Hollywood movie star with her wide-brimmed hat complete with a black veil, and a dress that looked like a cross between haute couture and a beekeeper's suit.

Star Sapphire, who was one of the school's resident fashionistas, gave the ensemble her highest compliment.

"I'd wear that," Bumblebee overheard her telling Cheetah as the two of them headed for the "Ask a Student Super Hero" seminar they were giving.

Everyone was so busy looking at the elegant woman that it was only as an afterthought that they noticed the young man lumbering three paces behind her. He wore glasses so thick that they made his eyes seem to bug out. He looked this way and that, waving to people as he passed.

"Oh, hey, hi!" he'd say, then chuckle like he had made a funny joke. His baggy black pants and striped black-and-yellow sweater made him look like a nerdy oversized bee.

When he saw Bumblebee, he lit up and nudged the elegant woman. Bumblebee heard him whisper, "Look, it's her!"

CHAPTER 24

Bumblebee had to smile. How could she not? Like most Supers, thanks to Harley's web channel, she was used to being recognized by fans. Still, she never tired of it. Some of her fellow students—especially those who had been born with powers—had gone to super-hero pre-K, super-hero elementary school, and super-hero middle school, so to them, being a Super was a way of life. A few sometimes felt burdened by fans, claiming they had no privacy. But not Bumblebee—at least, not in a big way. This was what she had always wanted, so to be recognized as a super hero was a big deal.

Ever thoughtful, Bumblebee always made sure to send thank-you notes to the Honey Bees when they sent her gifts, and had even been considering creating a Bumblebee website for fans who wanted to hear more from her.

The thought of her fans also brought her mind back to

the situation with the bees. She'd have to look into it more thoroughly as soon as—

"Excuse me," the young man in the black-and-yellow sweater said brightly. "Hi, hello! Bumblebee! I'm Cuckoo Bee!"

"Hello!" she said brightly as she strolled over to Cuckoo Bee. Cuckoo Bee grinned bashfully as he looked up at her.

"Well, hello to you," the elegant woman said. She looked down her nose at Bumblebee. "I am Beatriz, and Cuckoo Bee is my assistant."

"That's me!" Cuckoo Bee said, still waving as he hovered next to Beatriz.

"Are you thinking of sending your son or daughter to Super Hero High?" asked Bumblebee.

"My niece," Beatriz replied quickly. "A distant niece. She's currently off planet and couldn't make it; that's why I'm here."

Cuckoo Bee nodded. "Off planet!" he repeated. "Yes, she's off planet. Off planet, not here. Nope, not here. Don't see her."

When Beatriz glared at him, he immediately stopped talking and lowered his head.

"Not to worry. I'm sure you'll find a lot of good information to share with your niece," Bumblebee assured her. "The Flash will take you on a tour, and then Wonder Woman can answer any questions you might have. Or you can sit in on some of our classes." She handed the woman a holographic brochure that contained testimonials from current and past students. "And lots of guests are having fun in our 3-D Super Hero Video Booth, where you can try on different classic super-hero costumes and play with powers."

"NO!" Beatriz bellowed, before catching herself. She adjusted her hat. "Um, no, thank you," she said sweetly. "I'd rather not do any of that or have The Flash give me the tour. I want *you*."

Bumblebee hesitated. "You want me . . . to what?"

Beatriz adjusted her long black gloves. "I want you to give me a tour," she said.

"Oh, but I just coordinate the tours," Bumblebee explained. "We have lots of students who are wonderful tour guides—"

"I want YOU," Beatriz said firmly, like a woman who was used to getting her own way.

Hawkgirl flew up to them. She closed her wings and asked, "Is everything okay here?"

"My dear," Beatriz said, turning to Hawkgirl. The woman's movements were slow and graceful, like a ballet dancer's. "I'd like Bumblebee to give me the school tour, but she says she can't. Why is that?"

Hawkgirl looked at Bumblebee, who shrugged.

"Bumblebee," Hawkgirl volunteered, "why don't I take over tour coordination while you show them around?"

"Yay!" said Cuckoo Bee enthusiastically. "Bumblebee gives the tour! Bumblebee gives the tour! Bumblebee gives . . ." Beatriz shot him an angry glance and he stopped, though Bumblebee heard him whisper, ". . . the tour."

". . . and this is Mr. Fox's Weaponomics Lab," Bumblebee was saying as they neared the end of their tour.

"What's your weapon?" asked Beatriz. She didn't seem interested in the buildings or the new ballistics test field, which was equipped to simulate any state-of-the-art arsenal.

Bumblebee smiled. "I have sonic blasters, and I can fly," she said. "Plus, I can shrink and grow."

"Shrink and grow? Well, now, that's impressive," said Beatriz. "I'd like to see that!"

"Me too! Me too!" said Cuckoo Bee. "Please, Miss Bumblebee!"

Bumblebee had to laugh at his enthusiasm. "Oh, all right," she said. It wouldn't use up too much battery power if she did it just once. Bumblebee took a couple of steps back; then—WHOOSH!

"Where is she?" Cuckoo Bee gasped.

Her lighthearted laughter made the worried look on his

large face disappear. "I'm right here," Bumblebee said, flying circles around him.

"She's right here," Cuckoo Bee assured Beatriz.

"How does it work, this shrinking business?" Beatriz asked. "Did they teach it to you at school, or is it a power you were born with?"

"Neither," Bumblebee explained. "The super suit I created gives me the power to change size, and it also has the power to sustain my flight and strength."

"I can get small," Cuckoo Bee said. "Watch!" He blinked and seemed to be concentrating, then asked, "Am I small?"

"You're still the same," Beatriz snapped. "And that's not necessarily a good thing. Let's get out of here. I saw what I needed to see, and now there's work to be done." She paused for a moment and then turned and stared at Bumblebee. "I'll be seeing you later." She smiled in a way that gave the hero the creeps. "I'm sure of it."

As they left, Miss Martian suddenly appeared. "Something's not right with those two," she said.

"Oh, they're just a little odd," Bumblebee noted. "But then, so are a lot of others around here."

As if on cue, a green ostrich ran past, being followed by Cheetah, who was yelling, "Not funny, Beast Boy! I'm going to get you!"

CHAPTER 25

"And *that* is how you weaponize a pashmina scarf," Crazy Quilt said, bowing. When no one reacted, he waited and bowed again. Supergirl nudged Barda and the two began to clap until the whole room joined in. "Oh, stop! Stop!" The costume teacher waved his hands in the air. "You're embarrassing me!"

When everyone settled down, Crazy Quilt strolled back and forth along the large wooden worktables that flanked the runway cutting through the middle of the room. A wall of windows ensured that there was plenty of light to shine on Crazy Quilt and his students' creations.

"Today is all about problem solving," Crazy Quilt began. "Now, I know some of you think your super-hero costumes are perfect. But there is always room for improvement." He turned serious and raised one finger in the air, then slowly pointed to himself. "For example, look at me."

When Crazy Quilt leapt onto the runway, Big Barda

knew to start up the disco music that filled the room as he strutted up and down like the fashion icon he had once been. Bumblebee admired his dual-colored platform shoes, bell-bottom pants, and turquoise shirt with a wide collar and puffy sleeves.

When the music stopped, Crazy Quilt struck a pose, mimicking the image of his younger self splashed across the cover of *Super Hero Super Style* magazine. "Now, I know what you're all thinking," he said.

Bumblebee wondered if he did. She was thinking about her battery pack issue.

"You're thinking, 'He looks perfect,' " the teacher guessed. "Well, you're wrong, of course. Watch this!"

With a sweep of his arm, he made a light appear out of nowhere. Its flashing colors bounced off the walls, mesmerizing the students. "The flashlight was hidden in my sleeve," he explained. "However, would it be better if I had created a hidden compartment in the back of my belt? YES! The light would be easier to reach, and I wouldn't have to worry about it getting stuck in the swaying fabric."

Several Supers nodded. As usual, he was correct.

Crazy Quilt smiled. "So, as I was saying earlier, today is all about problem solving. I want you to come up with one thing that you would like help on to make your super suit the best it can be, and we will brainstorm together."

Supergirl was still having problems with her shoelaces coming untied, and Cheetah suggested triple knots. When Star Sapphire couldn't decide which outfit to wear since she had so many, Batgirl volunteered to develop a matrix so she could rotate her clothes without wearing the same one twice in a month. And Hal Jordan said he loved his green mask but sometimes he couldn't see. That was when Miss Martian suggested, rather shyly, that he cut his shaggy brown bangs.

When it was Bumblebee's turn, she knew what she wanted to discuss. "As most of you know, I've been having battery issues." Everyone nodded. At Super Hero High, there wasn't much that could be kept a secret. "So until I get my main battery pack issue sorted out, Batgirl and I have come up with an eco-friendly supplement—a solar battery." She smiled at Poison Ivy. "It was inspired by jars of sunshine I saw. But what I need has to be much smaller than a jar, lightweight, and worn outside my suit to maximize the sunlight."

Instantly, all hands and one snout went up in the air.

"How big is small?" asked Beast Boy in anteater form.

"Do you want it on the front or back of your super suit?" Hawkgirl said.

"Is this to blend in, accentuate, or be invisible?" Katana wondered aloud with her art pad and pencil in hand. She was already sketching.

It was Cyborg who suggested the photovoltaic module be miniaturized in Mr. Fox's lab.

Katana thought that by adding a micro panel similar to the one between Bumblebee's wings to the sonic blasters on her wrists, she would have more access points to gather sunlight.

Raven had noted that the material on the sleeves of Bumblebee's super suit could be coated with a heat protection film. "Even though the panels are harvesting and storing the sun's energy," she explained, "they might also work like a magnifying glass to make something melt or burn, and I'd hate for that to happen to you."

"Beast Boy, stop flittering around as a butterfly and get serious," Supergirl said as he made his way around the room.

"Hey, lady, I am being serious," he said. "Everyone knows that butterflies are great fliers."

"Wait!" Batgirl leapt up. She began typing so fast on her computer keyboard that Bumblebee thought she saw smoke coming out of it. "I've got it!"

"Got what?" Beast Boy asked, now back to a green teen.

"Biomimicry!" shouted Batgirl.

"Yes, biomimicry!" Beast Boy yelled. "Um, what is that, exactly?"

Batgirl explained to the class that biomimicry was a multidisciplinary approach to engineering in which science piggybacked off nature to create the most efficient devices.

As Batgirl went on, Bumblebee's mind began to whirl. *Of course!* she thought. The answer was right in front of her . . . in the shape of Beast Boy butterfly.

"The solar panels!" Bumblebee said in a rush of excitement. "Instead of isolating them to chips, we should mimic butterflies. Their wings are often iridescent—that is, they appear shiny when the light hits them. We can bank on this with my wings, because they would be the most efficient draw of sunlight and hence the perfect place for the solar panels. . . ."

"But what if they weren't just panels?" Hawkgirl asked excitedly. "What if the whole wing could absorb sunlight?"

"Shiny?" said Star Sapphire. "Like diamonds. We could use the strength of diamonds to fortify the panels. . . ."

"But where could we get diamonds?" Green Lantern asked.

All eyes turned back to Star Sapphire, who blinked innocently and looked up at the ceiling before letting go of a huge sigh and saying, "Okay, I may have a few that I can give up."

As the class talked excitedly about the possibilities, Waller stood at the back of the room. Before she left, she gave a nod of approval to Crazy Quilt, who was beaming.

CHAPTER 26

The Bat-Bunker wasn't big enough for all that had to be done, which meant that it was a busy night in Mr. Fox's Weaponomics Lab. Under Cyborg's direction, Supergirl was slicing the facets of the diamonds into sturdy microscopic cells with her heat vision. Bumblebee was reengineering the solar panels and fitting the diamond cells into the new wing configuration she had created.

On the other side of the lab, Ivy was creating a nonflammable nitrocellulose adhesive spray. As a big green woolly mammoth, Beast Boy was grinding leftover diamond bits into a fine powder in a mortar by using his muscular trunk to work the pestle. With his trunk doing all the work, Beast Boy's mouth was free to sing, "I'm the inspiration!"

Ivy poured the diamond powder into a large test tube with the micro solar cells and the nitrocellulose. She then handed it to Cyborg, who shook up the mixture at high speed with his bionic arm. Satisfied it was ready, Ivy filled up a high-intensity pressure sprayer with the solar solution. "Goggles on," she ordered. "Three, two, one . . . here I go!"

Everyone was giving Bumblebee looks of support as Ivy sprayed on layer after layer of the mixture. When the sprayer was empty, there was a chorus of oohs and aahs. Bumblebee's wings now took on a glittery golden glow.

"Test them," said Batgirl. "Do they feel heavier?"

Bumblebee flew around the room. "Only slightly," she reported. "But if this allows me to access the sun's energy to power my super suit, it's worth it!"

Batgirl was busy on her computer, inputting the details of the experiment. "Your wings are now lightweight solar panels. The diamonds will focus the sunlight and give your wings added strength," she said, looking at the statistics. "When they're fully charged, you'll have a good four hours. Plus, when you finish engineering that optimization program for your battle suit, you'll have even more time, depending on your flight speed, use of sonic blasters, and, of course, how often you shrink and grow."

"Absolutely," Bumblebee said happily. "I'll still need a backup battery pack for when there's no sunlight. But we can work on that later. There's no hurry."

The sneezing had taken on new life and would not let up. It was as if the world had a cold, although some places seemed to have been hit harder than others.

"The crops are failing," Poison Ivy reported from her greenhouse. "Not everywhere, but in enough places to warrant worry."

"Failing!" Jason Woodrue echoed as he stuck his head into the camera frame.

"Um, thank you, Jason," Ivy said. "I was just saying that."

"Failing!" he repeated, then smiled at her before stepping away. "Excuse me, sorry. This is *your* show."

Poison Ivy tried not to look at him staring at her, and continued, "Luckily, here in the greenhouse, all the plants are thriving, thanks to the ideal conditions we've been able to replicate."

"And thanks to Jason Woodrue," said Jason Woodrue as he held up a trowel in one hand and a red watering can in the other. "Thriving!"

After the show, which featured "Festive, Colorful Flowers from Hue to You," Batgirl, Bumblebee, and Beast Boy had a meeting. "I'm seriously concerned about what's going on with the honey," Bumblebee said.

"Me too," Batgirl replied. "And not just because of the paper we have to write."

"At first I thought the lack of honey was just an odd dry spell," Bumblebee said. "But my sources tell me it's everywhere now. And a lack of honey signals something even worse."

"*Achoo!*" Beast Boy let out a series of sneezes.

"Exactly!" said Bumblebee. "It's the pollen."

"The weird fake pollen," Ivy added as she joined them. "We've tried to investigate it, but—"

"It's affecting the crops," Beast Boy said. He had a tissue stuffed up each nostril. "At least, it seems like the culprit. But by the time the crops are failing, there's hardly any trace of the fake pollen left. And that makes it difficult to track it to its source."

"But the damage has been done, and that's why we're short on fruits and vegetables," Ivy went on.

"And honey," Bumblebee added. "The bees are being targeted in some regions, causing a honey shortage."

"I don't get it," said Beast Boy. "Why only in some places? Why the bees? What does this mean?"

"Bees are vital to our world's ecosystem," Bumblebee explained. "Most of our crops are pollenated by bees. Remember when I explained how bees visit flowers to collect nectar and pollen to make honey?"

"That's nice work if you can get it!" Beast Boy exclaimed.

Bumblebee went on, "By doing that, the bees spread pollen from plant to plant, helping those plants reproduce."

"So why the fake pollen?" Ivy asked.

"Wait," Beast Boy said, scratching his head. "Someone must be spreading it to confuse the bees. Instead of real pollen, they're attracted to the fake kind!"

"Exactly," Bumblebee agreed. "And this fake pollen makes the bees drowsy, so they don't visit as many plants or make honey for their hives to live on."

Poison Ivy jumped in: "That's why the flowers are all turning brown—not only does the fake pollen affect the bees, it affects the plants, too. Plus, the fake pollen is what's making everyone sneeze."

"Who could be behind this?" Bumblebee asked.

Beast Boy began to walk in circles. "I've got it!" he said, then sneezed. "Tissue companies!"

"Or a super-villain," Poison Ivy added.

"Or a honey company," Bumblebee said. "One that wants all the world's business. But then why would they hurt the bees?"

As they kept coming up with theories, the sneezing went on, the crops continued to fail, and there was no honey to be had anywhere.

While Batgirl was tracking the supply chains of tissue manufacturers, frozen and canned food companies, and any others who would profit from the damage caused by the fake pollen, Bumblebee was talking to her mom.

"A free vacation?" Bumblebee asked. "That sounds pretty cool."

"I know!" Ms. Andrena-Beecher said. "And we don't even remember entering. But you know your dad—he's always entering contests."

Bumblebee smiled. She did know. There was the time he came up with the jingle for Superior Sudsy Soap and won a lifetime supply. Or when he was closest in the Guess the Number of Jelly Beans contest at Benny's Donut House. Or when he entered the Bake a Better Bread contest and his honey-butter bread recipe won second place—Bumblebee had helped him with that one.

"So what's the prize this time?" Bumblebee asked.

"You're not going to believe it," her mother gushed. "An all-expenses-paid trip to Bialya!"

"Wow, that's amazing!" Bumblebee cried. "Um, where's Bialya?"

"We're not sure," Ms. Andrena-Beecher confessed. "But with the house still under construction, I think we've overstayed our visit with Cousin Keisha. Plus, it would be nice to get away for a bit. We'll call you when we get there."

"Have fun!" Bumblebee said. "Talk to you soon."

CHAPTER 27

Bumblebee was having trouble focusing. What she really wanted to do was test her solar battery wings, but with the pollen situation becoming more alarming, there was little time for that.

Wonder Woman and Supergirl were gathering samples from other parts of the world where the fruits and vegetables had stopped growing, and Hawkgirl was assisting Batgirl and Poison Ivy with more pollen testing. Bumblebee was charged with checking on the bee population—and she was distressed by what she saw. Everywhere, normally happy and busy bees were now drowsy and lethargic. Before she had a chance to process it all, the principal called her into her office.

"I heard from Kait's Pesty Pest Control Company," Waller said, setting down her heavy mug of double-caffeinated coffee. "Something very odd was discovered at your house. They couldn't reach your parents, so they called here. They'd like someone to meet them this afternoon." Before

Bumblebee could ask, Waller nodded. "Permission to leave campus," she said, adding, "And take a friend or two with you. With all this mystery about the fake pollen, I'd like to play it safe."

"Sure," Poison Ivy said to Bumblebee. "I'd like to know what happened to that tree, too."

"Do you need a ride?" Wonder Woman asked. "I was going to take my Invisible Jet for a test run. I want to see if I can break the sound barrier at twice the rate I did last time."

They were outside on the lawn near the Crystal Tower when several balls of fire arched across the sky, followed by a flurry of snowballs. "Heads up!" Wonder Woman called out as El Diablo and Frost continued their long-distance throwing contest from the far side of school.

"You two take the jet," Bumblebee said. "This is a great opportunity to test my new solar battery. Meet you there!"

So far, Bumblebee had gotten it to hold a full charge for almost four hours. However, her goal was a battery that could last for a full day or more without needing recharging. Still, four hours was better than three hours or two hours or nothing, she figured.

If felt so good to be flying again, swooping up and down, around the trees, past buildings.

"Hi, Bumblebee!" people called as she flew overhead.

"Hello!" she shouted down, thrilled to be in the air. Bumblebee looked at her watch. She had been flying for twenty minutes, but the sunlight had been hitting the battery pack, therefore charging it, and it was amassing more stored energy.

"How's it going?" a voice asked on her comm bracelet. Bumblebee laughed. "Great, Batgirl. Thanks for checking in. I'm going to power down to bee size now."

Wonder Woman and Poison Ivy were waiting. "What took you so long?" Ivy asked.

"Sorry!" Bumblebee said as they walked over to the Kait's Pesty Pest Control van. "I was flying and keeping an eye on my new battle suit's energy use versus its solar intake. Plus, flying at full speed again was so much fun, I sorta lost track of time."

"Been there, done that!" Wonder Woman said. "But now that you are here, let's check out this tree situation."

"You must be Karen Andrena-Beecher," the young woman in the blue lab coat called out as they rounded the corner of the house. "I'm Kait."

"Yes, I'm Karen, or you can call me Bumblebee," she answered.

Kait smiled. "Of course! I recognize you from *Harley's Quinntessentials*! And Wonder Woman!" She looked around. "And Poison Ivy! I love your new show *Greenhouse Hullabaloo.*"

"A pleasure to meet you," Poison Ivy replied, almost bashfully. All the attention she had been receiving from the web show had left her feeling a bit unsettled.

"Well, this is a great crew," Kait said.

"Excuse me, Kait," Bumblebee interrupted. "But there was something you wanted to show me?"

"Yes, yes! I've got some pretty weird findings, and I thought I should talk to someone in person about it," Kait answered.

Bumblebee could not contain her curiosity any longer. "Please, fill me in," she pressed.

Bumblebee could see that a new foundation for the house had been poured, and the wooden framing for the walls was almost finished.

"Over there," Kait said, pointing to the fallen Bee Tree. "It looks like a clean cut through the trunk. Bugs don't work like that. Especially termites, which are always our prime suspect when trees are destroyed."

Bumblebee studied the tree trunk and nodded. "You're right," she said. "I don't know of any termites that could cut a straight swath across the base of such a substantial tree."

Kait held up a clear tube with something moving inside. "I found these at the scene."

"Bees?" Bumblebee exclaimed. "I don't understand."

"Not just any bees," Kait informed them. "They're carpenter bees."

Bumblebee turned to Wonder Woman and Poison Ivy and explained, "Bees that are great at pollinating shallow flowers."

"Yes, but these are the *Xylocopa virginica* species," Kait noted. "They rob nectar by piercing the flowers, unlike most bees, which don't harm or destroy them. However, I believe these particular ones are mutants. Carpenter bees make nests by tunneling into wood. These not only tunneled, they sawed their way across the entire trunk of this tree until it fell over."

Bumblebee shuddered. Mutant bees attacking her lab? That seemed too odd to be a coincidence.

As Kait answered Wonder Woman's and Poison Ivy's questions, Bumblebee inspected the fallen Bee Tree. The caution tape was down. Remnants of her lab were scattered about, but it looked like most of her equipment had been destroyed in the fire. Picking up a stick, Bumblebee began to poke at the ashes, hoping she could find some things that hadn't been damaged.

There was no sign of the prototypes she had been working

on. Her entire spare super suit must have been ruined, along with the emergency battery packs. Bumblebee did manage to find a couple of unbroken beakers and three spools of wire, but surely there would have been more? Like spare parts. A computer mainframe. Some of the synthetic weave she'd made for creating new battle suits. She was starting to realize that it was looking less like her stuff had been destroyed, and more like it was . . . missing.

Then Bumblebee noticed something tucked into a knot in the tree. A note. It read:

> You have something I need, and I have something you want. And if we don't meet, the world will be worse for it. Directions ~~attacked~~ attached.
>
> P.S. If you ever want to see your parents again, do not tell anyone where you are going.

CHAPTER 28

"You take the bug samples to be analyzed," Bumblebee told Ivy. "Wonder Woman, please let Batgirl know the solar battery is working great. I'm going to hang out and visit the neighbors, but there's a glitch in my comm bracelet, so I'll be out of touch for a bit."

"Sure thing," Wonder Woman said. Bumblebee didn't like fibbing to her friends, but she wasn't staying behind to visit. No, she was going to follow the directions in the note and bring her parents back safely.

The note was written in childlike scrawl and hard to decipher. There was a map attached, but it didn't appear to be to scale and the coordinates were jumbled with arrows pointing this way and that. As Bumblebee took off, the sky began to get overcast. She worried about her solar panels, and kept trying to pierce through the clouds to get to the sunlight.

Because the map was so confusing, Bumblebee had

trouble staying on course. It didn't help that a storm was threatening—she felt heavy with dread as the clouds turned dark and the air thickened and cooled. Finally, Bumblebee recognized a mountain range in the distance. Just past it was the final destination—the X on the map. She took a deep breath. Her battery pack began to flicker. She had 23 percent power left.

Once she cleared the top of the jagged gray mountain range, the clouds parted enough to reveal a huge castle below. Bumblebee slowed. She couldn't believe her eyes. *Can this even be real?* she wondered. Bumblebee circled a few times, enough to get the lay of the land, then finally landed inside the massive dark and dreary estate.

The run-down castle looked like it might have been beautiful in another time, in another place. All around the crumbling palace was a blighted and desolate landscape. Bare trees, dried and hunched over, leaned against each other like weary skeletons. Flowers, brittle to the touch, gathered in clumps in what had most likely been a lavish flower bed in another life. Instead of green, all was gray. And the air. The air was so heavy she had to push through it, like wading through the water in a murky pond.

Bumblebee sneezed.

As she walked down the dirt path leading to the castle, the crunch of dead leaves announced her. Bumblebee turned off her battery to save energy. Above the heavy wooden door was a crest for "Honeycomb Hall." Bumblebee thought of calling Batgirl for backup, then remembered the ominous warning.

If you ever want to see your parents again, do not tell anyone where you are going.

Bumblebee wondered if her parents were inside. Who would do this, and why? Her heart raced.

The door creaked when she pushed it open. Bumblebee sneezed again. Apprehension took hold of her as she entered the cold and dark castle. It was cavernous, with a maze of rooms. Worn tapestries depicting staid royal families lined the walls. Everyone looked sad, even the dogs who sat at their masters' feet. White sheets over furniture looked like odd-shaped ghosts, and stained-glass windows were covered with a layer of dust.

At the far end of a narrow hallway lined with ancient medieval weapons, Bumblebee thought she saw a flicker of light from underneath a heavy velvet curtain. A familiar sound drew her toward it. It sounded like—could it be? The buzz of bees?

The closer Bumblebee got, the louder the sound. Only,

this buzzing wasn't the usual happy sound of bees visiting flowers and humming around their hives. No, this was a menacing, angry sound unlike anything she had ever heard before.

Bumblebee turned on her batteries, just in case. Then she took a deep breath and pulled back the curtain.

CHAPTER 29

In the shadows, an ornate gold throne encrusted with gems rested on a dais three steps up. On it sat a woman cloaked in black and yellow. A flowing robe was draped around her shoulders, and a crown of thorny black roses rested on her head. A veil hid her face, but Bumblebee could make out cruel eyes staring at her.

Hovering at the woman's side was someone Bumblebee was surprised to see. When he waved, she waved back, though not with nearly as much enthusiasm.

"Cuckoo Bee?" she asked, though she knew the answer to her question.

"Yup! It's me. Hi, Bumblebee!" he said.

The woman did not move. Bumblebee wondered if perhaps she was also a victim of whoever had kidnapped her parents. Suddenly, Bumblebee noticed that the buzzing had ramped down to a low but still-menacing sound, like a circular saw. She turned to find swarms of bees lining the walls in neat rows.

The room resembled a medieval museum filled with eclectic military antiques, including a rusted suit of armor and an old-fashioned deep-sea-diving suit with a metal helmet. On one wall, flanking a massive coat-of-arms tapestry, were crossbows, battle-axes, spears, and lances. In the corner was a heavy metal cannon with its fuse still intact. What looked like perfume atomizers, along with several globes and magnifying glasses, rested on a desk made of tortoiseshell, pewter, brass, and bronze. On another wall was a yellowing poster of a scenic village, with the message "Visit beautiful Bialya, for the vacation of a lifetime."

Bialya! That was where her parents had "won" a vacation to, Bumblebee realized. She startled when the woman on the throne spoke.

"Aren't you going to curtsy to your queen?" the woman asked, lifting her veil.

Bumblebee's eyes narrowed. Of course it was her. After all, Cuckoo Bee was there, wasn't he? "Beatriz, what do you want?" Bumblebee's voice was tight.

"*Queen* Beatriz," the woman replied, haughtily correcting the young super hero. "Though I prefer to go by Queen Bee. Now curtsy!"

Bumblebee stood tall. "You are not my queen," she said. "I demand to know what you've done with my parents!"

Queen Bee laughed. "Oh, child. You demand to know? No one makes demands of me. Calm down. Would you like some tea . . . with honey?" She turned to Cuckoo Bee. "Tea and honey, now!"

"Yes, yes, my queen," her assistant said. Before he left, he whispered to Bumblebee, "Nice to see ya again!"

"Where are my parents?" Bumblebee asked, her voice rising. She clenched her fists and raised her arms slowly, her sonic blasters ready on full charge.

"Royal Army," Queen Bee said, regally motioning to the killer bees who buzzed nearby, "stand ready in case our guest has any plans to attack." She turned back to Bumblebee. "Your parents, they're fine, they're safe, they're on vacation," she added dismissively. "It's you I want to talk about."

"I need proof that my parents are okay," Bumblebee said, standing her ground.

Cuckoo Bee returned carrying a tray heavy with cups of tea, a silver chalice overflowing with honey, and lightly toasted orange-honey scones. He set it down on a small table next to Queen Bee.

"Bumblebee, we need to talk," she said, pouring what seemed like an endless stream of honey into her tea, then stirring it slowly. The queen closed her eyes as she took a long sip before setting the delicate white china teacup down and saying, "My, but that is delicious. Wouldn't you like some?"

Bumblebee bit her lip. How long had it been since she'd

had honey? The honey before her was so sweet she could smell it. The golden hues seemed to illuminate the chalice, and the tops of the scones had been drizzled with caramelized honey.

"My parents!" Bumblebee said, remembering why she was there. She chided herself for letting herself be distracted by honey. "I need proof."

Queen Bee picked up a pastry and took a small bite. "Ah, Cuckoo Bee bakes the best orange-honey scones," she said.

Cuckoo Bee, who was pacing back and forth behind the throne, stopped to blush. "It's true," he said. "I like to bake."

"SILENCE!" Queen Bee snapped. "No one said you could talk."

He lowered his head in shame. "Bad Cuckoo Bee, bad, bad Cuckoo Bee," he said, fleeing into a corner and putting himself in time-out.

"All right, here's the proof of your parents' safety," Queen Bee said, sounding resigned. She pressed a button on the armrest of her throne and an image was projected onto the wall. It was of Mr. and Ms. Andrena-Beecher.

CHAPTER 30

Bumblebee's mother and father were making their way down a dark, damp alley, accompanied by mutant humanoid bees from the queen's Royal Army.

"Are you sure they're tour guides?" Ms. Andrena-Beecher whispered to her husband. "They don't say much other than *bzzzzzz*."

"What else would they be?" asked Mr. Andrena-Beecher. "And the way they are sticking to us is marvelous. They don't want us to get lost."

Ms. Andrena-Beecher smiled warmly at her husband. He had a habit of getting lost, especially when they were on vacation.

"Mom! Dad!" Bumblebee yelled. "Are you okay?"

Queen Bee took another bite of scone, then dabbed at the corner of her mouth with a red silk napkin. "They can't hear you," she said, sounding bored. "I've got a BotBee with a camera on them. But see, I'm true to my word. Not only are they safe, but they think they are on vacation."

"You'd better not harm them!" Bumblebee's eyes darkened.

Queen Bee ignored her, instead muting the sound on the BotBee's live feed while the images still played. She poured more honey into her tea. "I have an unlimited supply," she boasted. "The world's finest honeybees work for me."

"All the bees work for her!" said a voice in the corner.

Queen Bee shook her head. "Not yet, but they will," she said. "Soon."

Bumblebee looked to where Cuckoo Bee was still in time-out. He spoke facing the wall. "Our queen used BotBees—you know, robots—to shower her pollen all over. It made the honeybees sleepy," he said, yawning. "She's so smart!"

"True," Queen Bee said, trying to sound modest. "Though you teens keep calling it 'fake pollen,' when I prefer 'slumber dust.' If all goes according to plan, I'll have my army of BotBees continue blanketing the far corners of the planet with it, and you know what that means, right?"

Bumblebee nodded. If all the bees were disabled, then they could not pollinate. Without bees as pollinators, the world's food sources would eventually vanish, thus destroying all life on the planet.

"Why do you want to do this?" Bumblebee asked. With only a little battery power left, she knew she'd have to use it judiciously to survive.

"Control!" Cuckoo Bee shouted excitedly from his corner.

"SILENCE!" Queen Bee ordered. As Cuckoo Bee quaked, she continued. "Why should I do any work when I'm smart enough to have others work for me, like you'll be doing soon? My BotBees did an excellent job disseminating my slumber dust. Of course, they didn't spread it everywhere. Just in enough places to catch your attention. Plus, they didn't get near my personal crop of the world's most gorgeous flowers. Only the best honeybees in the world have access to them. How else would I get all this?"

With her majestic robe trailing behind her, Queen Bee strolled over to a large metal door and opened it. Bumblebee gasped. She had never seen so much honey in her life.

"So this is what it's all about?" Bumblebee said as she gawked at the rows and rows of honey jars. "Owning all the honey in the world?"

Queen Bee returned to her throne. "It's not just about the honey—sweet as it is. It's about *taking over* the world. And, Bumblebee, that's where you come in. . . ."

PART
THREE

CHAPTER 31

Bumblebee was taken aback. "What does any of this have to do with me?"

"It has everything to do with you," Queen Bee said. She motioned to her killer bees on the other side of the room. "My Royal Army bees brought me the tech from your lab before they destroyed it. But even after tearing everything apart, I couldn't figure all of it out. Then I realized: Why should I work at this when you can do it for me? So"—she leaned forward and stared hard at Bumblebee—"tell me your secret."

"Tell her, or she'll get mad!" Cuckoo Bee whispered loudly from time-out. "It's no fun when she gets mad."

Bumblebee struggled to digest the information. "You want my secret so you can shrink?"

Queen Bee let go of a long laugh. "No, not me. Why would I ever want to get small? As it is, I'm undefeatable. I'm brilliant, I got top grades in school, and I've got venomous stingers and my slumber dust."

Bumblebee could feel anger rising inside her. "Your slumber dust is crippling the world by killing all the crops!"

Queen Bee blushed. "Why, so nice of you to notice," she said. "Disable, distract, and conquer. As for me shrinking—no, no, no, no, no, I have no desire to get small. I want your technology so I can reverse it!"

"What?" Bumblebee asked. Was she hearing correctly? "You want to get . . . bigger?"

For a brief second, Bumblebee was distracted by the images of her parents on the wall. They looked lost. She noticed that the number of "tour guides" seemed to have thinned out.

"Not me, silly," Queen Bee said, looking amused. "My Royal Army. Imagine giant mutant killer bees. They're a threat when they're small, but as giants, they'd be a conquering force capable of subduing the world!"

"And what about your BotBees?" Bumblebee asked. "Them too?"

"Them? No," Queen Bee said with a dismissive wave. "BotBees are servants, not warriors."

"I'm not sure I understand," said Bumblebee. Evil could be so confusing sometimes.

"Argggh!" Queen Bee cried, leaping up from her throne. "Don't they teach you anything at Super Hero High? Logic this out: one, my Royal Army is made up of giant mutant bees; two, they will take over the world; and three, everyone works for me, their *wonderful* queen. Is that so hard to fathom?"

On the wall, Bumblebee could see her parents. The BotBee was still videoing them, but they had somehow become separated from the Royal Army. *Are they lost or have they escaped?* she wondered. *And either way, are they in any less danger?*

Pleased with her own diabolical plan, Queen Bee was still rambling on. "As you know, each beehive has its own queen. But with me in charge, I will not only be the queen of all the bees, I'll be *queen of the world*!"

Watching her parents, Bumblebee felt a slight twinge of hope. With her mom and dad safely away from the Royal Army, she could fight Queen Bee!

"Did you like what you saw at Super Hero High?" Bumblebee asked, stalling while she formulated a plan.

A slash of a smile crossed Queen Bee's face. "It hasn't changed all that much. . . . I used to be a student there."

"But you took a tour . . . ," Bumblebee began. She stopped herself. "You were there to—"

"Meet you," Queen Bee confirmed, nodding. "Why would I need to find out anything about Super Hero High? I practically ruled it when I was there."

"Tell me more about it," Bumblebee goaded her. She needed time to think.

"Ah, the memories," Queen Bee said wistfully.

"So you went to my school?" Bumblebee asked.

"No, *you* go to *my* school," Queen Bee snapped. She leaned back in her throne. "I was just like you once, only smarter. You do your school assignments yourself, but I got others to do mine for me. And it was at Super Hero High that I learned to love bees!"

Thanks to a BotBee camera, Bumblebee could see her parents wandering alone on the streets of Bialya, looking lost and worried. But at least this seemed to confirm that they had become separated from the Royal Army "tour guides"!

Queen Bee was lost, too . . . in her own story. "I was so in love with bees," she was reminiscing. "Everything bees! Beehives! Honeycombs! Spelling bees! Anything bees! I started the Bee All That You Can Bee Club. Is that still there?" She didn't wait for Bumblebee's answer. "After I left Super Hero High, I knew that it was my mission to protect the bees. I mean, there is so much adversity out there, one needs to be careful."

As Queen Bee continued, Bumblebee turned on her comm bracelet. She tried to relay a message to Batgirl with her coordinates, speaking softly and quickly, before turning it off again to conserve power.

". . . so I began protecting the bees," Queen Bee was saying. "Taking them under my wing. Making sure they weren't working too hard, seeing that they had plenty of nectar, as only I could. After all, no one cares for bees more than me." She leaned forward. "No one does more for the bees than I do, and they should be grateful for that!"

"I'm grateful, er . . . I think," said Cuckoo Bee from his dark corner. He looked at Bumblebee and shrugged.

Queen Bee was now pacing and ranting as her Royal Army swarmed this way and that, careful to stay out of her way. "I finally realized that I was a queen. *The* queen. And what does a queen do? She *rules*!"

And with that, Queen Bee spun a globe of the world that was at her fingertips. Her laughter filled the halls of the castle. She was obviously absorbed in the vision of her own greatness.

Bumblebee knew that now was her chance. She needed to spring into action before Queen Bee realized that Mr. and Ms. Andrena-Beecher's guards were nowhere to be seen. She turned on her power. There was less than fourteen minutes of energy left. As Bumblebee felt the welcome surge of her super suit powering up, one of the Royal Army bees startled her.

"Knock, knock! Who's there?" a familiar voice asked. "Bee. Bee who? Look who's *bee*-hind you!"

CHAPTER 32

"*Beast Boy?*" Bumblebee whispered, wide-eyed. Never in her entire life had she been so happy to see a green killer bee.

"Batgirl got your message," he said. "But it was all garbled and the location coordinates didn't transmit clearly, so we split up to look for you. The reception here is horrible!"

"Is everyone outside?" Bumblebee asked hopefully. Queen Bee was now staring out the window and pontificating about why it should be an honor for everyone to have her in charge.

Beast Boy bee shook his head. "Waller put most of the Supers out on natural-disaster detail. They're using what we learned to wash away the fake pollen to get the world's ecosystems back on track." He pointed to Queen Bee. "Is *she* serious?"

Bumblebee nodded. "Sadly, yes. Tell me about the rest of the Supers, but hurry!"

"Supergirl and Wonder Woman are diverting rainstorms

to farms, with Thunder and Lightning using their powers to help keep the storms manageable," Beast Boy said in a rush. "Frost is harnessing ice from an avalanche, and El Diablo's melting it to feed into rivers. It's natural disasters to the rescue, but once the Supers are done, they'll be headed here. That is, if they can find us."

Bumblebee smiled. Leave it to the Supers of Super Hero High to save the day. But now it was her turn. "Beast Boy," she said quickly, "I want to take on Queen Bee. But those guys"—she motioned to the Royal Army, who were now hovering near the doorways—"are in my way. Can you distract them, get them out of here?"

"Can I?" asked Beast Boy, his eyes sparkling with mischief. "You just try and stop me!"

"Oh, and there's something else I need you to do," Bumblebee told him.

Queen Bee had worn herself out and was now resting on her throne. "I'm going to get your secret," she warned Bumblebee as her attention shifted back to the young hero. "But first, it's time for my afternoon honey break. Cuckoo Bee! Honey. Here! Now!"

Cuckoo Bee ran to the vault and brought out heavy glass

jars of honey. He handed them to his queen, who drank them one after the other.

Bumblebee nodded to Beast Boy. "Go," she said.

"Gone!" he said as he turned into a wasp. "Hey, Royal Army killer bee dudes and dudettes, look at me! I'm one of you," Beast Boy wasp shouted as he buzzed circles around them.

As the Royal Army began to give chase, Beast Boy wasp taunted and teased, and turned off the live video feed of Bumblebee's parents, as she had asked him to do. "You wasps aren't fast enough to catch me!" he yelled. "Oops, I meant killer bees, or are you bozo bees?"

Queen Bee looked up from a jar of honey. "What is going on?" she demanded. By then, Beast Boy had led the Royal Army away from the throne room and down a corridor.

"Don't listen to her," Bumblebee was saying to Cuckoo Bee as he retreated to his corner. "I know you're not a bad guy. Stand up to her, I'll protect you!"

His big eyes began to water. "You will?" he asked.

"I promise," Bumblebee said.

"YOU!" Queen Bee yelled, pointing at Bumblebee. "This is your doing! Well, enough of me being nice to you. If you don't respond to my invitations, I'll just have to take what I need, and that means your super suit!"

Cuckoo Bee was trembling.

"Cuckoo Bee, get over here!" Queen Bee ordered.

He looked at Bumblebee, then Queen Bee, then back at Bumblebee. Cuckoo Bee lowered his head and mumbled, "I am sorry."

"Sorry for what?" Queen Bee spat.

"For this," he said.

Bumblebee watched Queen Bee's anger rise as Cuckoo Bee abandoned her, scurrying from the throne room in such a hurry he ran into the wall. He picked himself up and dashed out of sight. "He's an idiot," Queen Bee said as she turned to face Bumblebee. "But he's my cousin's son, so I had to give him a job. Anyway, now it looks like it's just you and me."

"As it should be," Bumblebee said, stepping into fighting stance. "Let's get this over with!"

Beast Boy wasp flew out a keyhole at the far end of the hall and into what was left of the once-impressive gardens—with the Royal Army right behind him. It was now raining, and the killer bees were more than a hundred strong, but Beast Boy wasn't worried.

"Look, I'm a sparrow!" he yelled. He was so busy laughing that he didn't realize he was headed straight toward the tall garden wall. Before he could fly over it, the Royal Army surrounded him. The killer bees moved in slowly and deliberately for the attack.

"Uh-oh," Beast Boy said. "Gee, what's a bird to do?" He smiled and added, "Oops, did I say 'bird'? I'm an armadillo!"

The killer-bee stings were no match for Beast Boy armadillo's hard shell. "You're tickling me! You're tickling me!" he shouted as he rolled around on the ground. "I know, let's play a game called 'Who's Beast Boy Now?'"

As he ran around the expansive grounds, Beast Boy morphed into a honey badger who was also indifferent to beestings. "This is fun!" he shouted, before turning into a bear.

CHAPTER 33

No one was laughing inside the castle. Bumblebee had never been more serious in her life. The vault to the queen's massive honey collection remained open, the golden glow of the jars of honey spilling out into the throne room. But all Bumblebee could focus on was the evil queen standing before her.

Queen Bee stepped down from her throne and made her way slowly toward Bumblebee, who was clenching and unclenching her fists to loosen up. Katana had taught her, "In order to fight to the best of your best ability, instead of rushing . . . slow down." Wonder Woman had said, "Don't use everything you have all at once." And Batgirl had insisted, "Even without the battery, you're a formidable opponent. Never forget that."

Formidable opponent or not, Bumblebee now only had a few precious minutes left in her battery pack, and she was determined to take Queen Bee out in that time. She calculated how long each of her defensive and offensive moves would take, parsing out her power in seconds. Rising two feet off the ground, Bumblebee strategically positioned herself in front of her opponent. It wasn't enough to be strong, or to have a weapon like the sonic blasters; you had to know how to use your powers wisely.

Bumblebee looked around the room for places she could hide should she need to shrink. The diving suit cast a long shadow on the floor. Wait! A shadow? Bumblebee smiled. She knew what that meant. The sun was finally starting to break through the clouds. Without a light source, there would have been no shadow. Bumblebee glanced outside and spotted a green bear lumbering around with a jar of honey stuck on one paw and swatting the Royal Army away with the other.

"You refuse to try my honey, but how about this?" a voice said.

It was Queen Bee. Bumblebee turned around, but it was too late! Before she could defend herself, the queen grabbed an atomizer from her desk and sprayed her slumber dust in Bumblebee's face. "If that's not enough," Queen Bee asked mockingly, "then how about another helping?"

Her evil laughter rang through Honeycomb Hall as she reached for another atomizer and emptied a big blast of slumber dust in Bumblebee's direction. Instantly, Bumblebee shrank down and flew behind Queen Bee to evade the gas, knowing that this would drain her battery even faster. She had weighed the odds and figured that if she was sneezing nonstop, it would affect her ability to fight. And right now, she needed to be prepared for battle.

"You can't hide from me," Queen Bee said. "If anyone knows bees, it's me! I will rule them, all of them, especially *you!*"

Still sneezing and small, Bumblebee circled Queen Bee's head. When the queen swatted at her, Bumblebee grew big and knocked the queen down with her sonic blasters. In a heartbeat, Queen Bee rose. She ripped off her veil, revealing a face etched with rage.

"Take THAT!" Queen Bee shouted, firing a round of lethal stingers from under her flowing sleeves.

Bumblebee flew and dodged the first set, but one from the second round nicked her and she fell to the ground, quickly tucking into a roll and jumping up again. She was thankful her super suit was reinforced with synthetic para-aramid fibers that enabled it to deflect oncoming projectiles. Still, her shoulder hurt where the stinger had hit. But that only made Bumblebee more determined to fight.

As she flew around the room to shake off the pain, the vault of honey beckoned.

"I see you staring at my treasure," Queen Bee said haughtily. "I'll share with you—if you share with me. Just give me the secrets of your super suit, and I'll put you in charge of my Royal Army. Plus, you'll have all the honey you can eat!"

"No, thank you," Bumblebee said. She raised her blasters, aimed at Queen Bee, and fired. The momentum pushed her backward into a metal shield on the wall. The clang echoed around the room.

Queen Bee took cover behind her massive throne, which deflected the blasts, sending them ricocheting off the ancient weapons of war that lined the walls. Some of the blasts hit jars of honey in the vault, shattering them.

"That wasn't nice," Queen Bee warned. "Now that Cuckoo Bee has run off, who will clean up that mess? Oh, wait, I know! Karen Andrena-Beecher will. Because once I have Bumblebee's super suit, she won't be a super hero. No, she'll just be some kid who's going to need a job."

As Bumblebee continued to blast Queen Bee, her battery warning light went from green to yellow, signaling that she was going to lose power soon.

"How's about a little more achoo for you?" the queen asked, reaching for another atomizer of slumber dust.

Bumblebee ducked and avoided the fake pollen. As she did so, she felt herself starting to weaken: her super suit began to automatically power down. The red light was now blinking! Bumblebee had less than one minute of energy left before she became powerless.

"You don't scare me!" Bumblebee shouted, even though

she felt fear in the pit of her stomach. She flew over to the vault and began tossing jars of honey like missiles at Queen Bee, creating a sticky mess around the throne.

"Hey!" Queen Bee shouted. She took aim at Bumblebee, ready to shoot another dose of fake pollen.

Then, with only seconds to spare, Bumblebee shrank down to bee size and flew into the round metal helmet of the diving suit right before Queen Bee's slumber dust would have hit her.

Buzzing inside the suit, Bumblebee screwed her eyes shut. *Ten . . . nine . . . eight . . .* She didn't have much time before she lost all power! *Seven . . .* She took a deep breath and focused with all her might. *Six . . . five . . .* Bumblebee knew what she had to do. *Four . . . three . . .*

CHAPTER 34

Her heart raced. With merely seconds left before she'd lose power, bee-sized Bumblebee rose inside the metal diving helmet, pushing against it so that it lifted off the suit when she did. She took a big breath; then, with all her might, she flew toward the window. Queen Bee stopped screaming and stared at what looked like a bowling ball soaring through the air . . . then shattering the glass.

When the diving helmet struck the ground outside, Bumblebee was tossed around until it rolled to a stop. Gasping for air, and with a huge headache, she crawled out, feeling battered and weak. The grass was wet, and the sunlight felt warm. Bumblebee managed to sit up and looked around. The rain had cleared the slumber dust, and the sun was shining.

There was no time to lose. Bumblebee spread her wings. With zero power left, she needed to absorb as much sunlight as she could to recharge her solar panels. Luckily, the new wings were fast-absorbing. In the distance, she could see an army of killer bees being chased back into the castle by a green skunk.

Bumblebee hoped her juice pack was back to full force before—

"Ah, there you are, you little pest," Queen Bee said, looking down at tiny Bumblebee. The queen was dripping with honey. "It was nice knowing you. And as for the secret to your super suit and shrinking abilities, well, I've observed and studied you enough to know I can probably figure this out on my own. Just how hard could it be?"

With that, Queen Bee gave an evil laugh as she lifted one of her pointy-toed shoes to crush Bumblebee.

In an instant, Bumblebee grew big, grabbed the shoe, and rolled over, tossing Queen Bee to the ground in the process. Leaves and dirt stuck to the queen. Bumblebee leapt up and aimed her blasters at her opponent, but before she could fire, Queen Bee spat, "You may have won the first round, but I will win the second!" From beneath her sleeve, she unleashed a stinger point-blank at Bumblebee.

Though the super suit was too strong to be penetrated, the stinger still struck her with such force that Bumblebee was knocked down.

"Royal Army," Queen Bee ordered as she swiftly retreated behind Honeycomb Hall, "I need you NOW!"

Bumblebee stood up, twirling to make sure the warm

sunlight hit her wings from every angle. It would do her no good to go after Queen Bee while her energy was depleted. When she shaded her eyes, Bumblebee spotted the Royal Army swarming toward their queen. A green skunk was yelling after them, "Scaredy-cats!"

Bumblebee checked her battery. She was now up to 20 percent power. When that doubled, she decided, it would be time to stop Queen Bee once and for all.

The Royal Army was lined up in front of their queen. She revealed a small black box. Bumblebee knew it couldn't be good as Queen Bee pressed a red button on the top of it.

"Too late," she said, beaming at Bumblebee. "By tinkering with your shrinking technology, I've reversed it. It was simple, really. And now a dozen of my best Royal Army killer bees will soon become a very, very BIG problem for you and your friends!"

"Making things bigger can make them more unstable," Bumblebee warned. "Please. It might be dangerous for your bees!"

"They are mine to do with as I command," Queen Bee said, laughing. "It's possible that there may be some technical difficulties, but there's only one way to find out, right?"

Bumblebee's eyes grew wide. Slowly, one by one, a dozen soldiers in the Royal Army began to grow. Suddenly, a familiar figure appeared at her side.

"Get away!" Bumblebee shouted. "Cuckoo Bee, get out of here."

"And go where?" he asked. "I want to help."

"Then go get help," Bumblebee said. "You can do it! Cuckoo Bee, go for help."

"As if he can help anyone," Queen Bee scoffed as he ran off. "He's a dolt. However, *I* am a genius. Just look at my magnificent army!"

Just then, a green bear lumbered past. "Excuse me," he said, oblivious to the giant bees now awaiting their orders. "I was looking for a snack. Unless, of course, there's a battle to fight."

"You want a battle?" Queen Bee asked Beast Boy bear. "I'll give you a battle like you've never seen before!"

CHAPTER 35

The killer bees kept growing until they were the size of rhinos. To see them floating in the air would be at once impressive and intimidating to most, but not to Bumblebee. *Bigger is not better,* she thought.

"I guess I don't need you after all," Queen Bee said, waving her arms dramatically.

"You still don't know my secret to shrinking . . . or growing big," Bumblebee warned her. "Without the right program and settings, the results of altering their size could be disastrous!"

"I'll take my chances. Plenty more bees where they came from," Queen Bee said haughtily. "Now I'm off to conquer the world."

"No way!" said Beast Boy, back to being a boy. "We're gonna stop you."

"Are you still here?" Queen Bee asked, not even attempting

to stifle her laugh. "That's the funniest thing I've heard all week. You two and who else will stop me and my Royal Army?"

Bumblebee looked toward the castle. She smiled when she saw Cuckoo Bee's reflection in one of the leaded glass windows. "Who else will stop you and your Royal Army?" she asked. "I'll show you."

Behind Bumblebee, over the wall of Honeycomb Hall, rose an army of super heroes from Super Hero High, with Cuckoo Bee sitting alongside Wonder Woman in her Invisible Jet, leading the way.

"Hi, Queen Bee," Cuckoo Bee said, waving. "Uh, I'm with them now!"

Queen Bee's eyes narrowed and her lips pursed into a sour expression. "Army," she ordered, "get them!"

Instantly a battle raged, with Queen Bee's giant killer bees leading the Royal Army on one side, and several Supers on the other. Wonder Woman began lassoing the giant bees. Batgirl was on the ground, analyzing their flight patterns, calculating their next moves, and relaying that information to the Supers in the air.

Supergirl took on two giant killer bees at once. Her speed and strength overwhelmed them as she flew in circles, creating a vortex that spun them dizzy. Barda batted two more over the castle wall with her Mega Rod.

As Queen Bee shouted out orders to the giant killer bees, Bumblebee flew at her, grabbed the control box, then tossed it to Batgirl and shouted, "Reprogram this!"

Bumblebee turned to Beast Boy, who nodded back to her. "We got this covered," he told his friend. "You do what you need to do."

While The Flash taunted a duo of giant bees into chasing him, Frost lay in wait. Just as The Flash jetted past, she leapt into their path. "Not so fast," she said, freezing both. The ice-cold giant bees landed on the ground with a thud.

Harley Quinn, who had a video camera in one hand and her mallet in the other, was cheerfully multitasking. "Hey, *Harley's Quinntessentials* fans, while Poison Ivy is busy regenerating the world's flowers to grow and produce much-needed real pollen, here at Honeycomb Hall, we're having an epic battle!"

As she was talking, three giant killer bees headed straight at her. "**WOWZA**, you don't want to do that," Harley shouted gleefully, cartwheeling end over end in a series of forward flips. She used her momentum as she brought her mallet down, scattering the three killer bees. "One! Two! Three! They're out!"

As the fight raged on, with Supers versus giant killer bees and small Royal Army bees, Big Barda spied a frightened Cuckoo Bee cowering behind a rosebush. She rushed over to him.

"I'm scared," he said mournfully. "This is all my fault."

"You did good," Barda told him. "Don't worry, we'll protect you."

Back in the throne room, another battle was about to commence. But there were no cameras or armies or battalions of super heroes here.

"Nice of you to agree to meet me alone," Bumblebee said.

"Hurry, hurry, we'll need to hurry. I'll do away with you and then I need to get back to my army," Queen Bee said dismissively. "You've been a pest for far too long."

Bumblebee began to circle Queen Bee, who stood before her throne. The floor was sticky with honey, and shards of broken glass were everywhere. Sunlight streamed in through the windows, now that the rain had washed away the dirt. With each second, Bumblebee could feel her battery pack gaining more power.

Despite the roars and cries of battle outside, inside, the room was eerily quiet. Queen Bee got into fighting position. Bumblebee took a stance, raising her arms and aiming her sonic blasters at Queen Bee.

"I have my powers back online," Bumblebee warned her nemesis.

"Good thing," Queen Bee said. "Because without them,

you're just plain old Karen Andrena-Beecher, super-hero wanna*bee*."

A troubled look passed across Bumblebee's face.

Queen Bee's lip curled into a sneer. There was an evil glint in her eyes. "Oh, yes, that's right. Everyone knows that without your super suit, you're just another little girl pretending to be a super hero. I'm surprised Waller even let you into Super Hero High. My, my, how the standards have dropped."

Bumblebee's jaw clenched.

"You are nothing without your super suit," Queen Bee taunted. *"NOTHING!"*

The jab of Queen Bee's words pierced Bumblebee. For the first time since she'd gotten to Honeycomb Hall, serious doubt washed over her. Was she just playing super hero? That was the question she had been asking herself for weeks. Bumblebee looked at her power-control panel. The light was green, meaning she was charged up with energy and ready to use the full force of her resources.

Queen Bee was still smirking. "Am I right?" she asked. "Isn't it true you are nothing without your super suit?"

Bumblebee let the question play out in her brain. Finally, she took in a deep breath as her eyes narrowed. "You are wrong," Bumblebee told the queen. And with that, she turned her power off.

CHAPTER 36

"**S**eriously, you're not using your battle suit?" Queen Bee said, laughing. "And I thought that shape-shifting Beast Boy was the crazy one."

"You know Beast Boy?" Bumblebee asked, surprised.

"I've kept tabs on all you Supers," Queen Bee boasted. "But, oh, you two. You're delusional, and he's nothing more than a green goof-off—and certainly no match for me. In my day . . ."

As Queen Bee droned on, Bumblebee's quick mind allowed her to take inventory of the room. Within seconds, she had mapped the surroundings and formulated a plan. Slowly, Bumblebee backed up, then grabbed one of the heavy metal shields off the wall.

"What!" Queen Bee cried. She raised her arm and shot stingers at Bumblebee, who used the shield the deflect them.

As stinger after stinger pelted the shield, Bumblebee headed toward the corner. Once there, she crouched behind the iron cannon, pushing it toward the honey vault and pocketing a magnifying glass from the desk as she passed.

"This isn't even a fair battle," Queen Bee said, sounding bored. "I'm royalty, and you, you're just a regular girl—and not a very smart one, at that. If you think you can best me with a rusted old cannon, have at it."

Bumblebee grabbed a jar of honey off the vault shelf and placed it in the cannon. Quickly, she held the magnifying glass up to the window and watched as the sunlight lit the taper of the cannon. Soon the sizzle of the burn could be heard in the throne room.

Queen Bee rose to fly toward Bumblebee, but Bumblebee was ready for her. She picked up a crossbow and tried to remember what Arrowette had taught her about taking aim. Holding the bow parallel to the ground, and anticipating her opponent's velocity, she shot at Queen Bee, who had to duck to avoid getting hit. Then Bumblebee aimed the cannon. With a powerful BOOM, the honey jar shot out and struck its target dead center, knocking Queen Bee to the ground.

Sticky with honey and shards of glass, Queen Bee rose again, angrier than before. Then BOOM! Another honey cannonball struck her, and another and another.

Like a machine, Queen Bee kept moving forward, bent on exacting revenge on Bumblebee. "Karen, little Karen Andrena-Beecher, you are no match for me," Queen Bee taunted, but she was wobbling from the impact of the cannons. "I'm going to bring you down, and then use your technology to bring the world to its knees, and all will bow to me!"

Bumblebee went to grab another jar of honey and was surprised to find there were none left.

"Oh dear," Queen Bee said with false sweetness. "Well, so much for that little plan."

"Not quite," Bumblebee said. "I'm not finished with you yet."

"Ah, but I am finished with you," Queen Bee said, swatting the old iron cannon away. Her other arm came up. Her blaster was filled with slumber dust—and it was *not* set to stun. "*Nighty-night, sweet Bumblebee!*"

Bumblebee grabbed an ancient metal spear. As Queen Bee flew at her, she hesitated. Not because she was scared, but because in the span of less than two seconds, she was accessing her knowledge of math and aerodynamics to calculate her enemy's speed and to target the exact right moment to throw the spear with the perfect velocity.

"NOW!" Bumblebee said to herself. The spear sailed through the air and hit her target!

"WHAT?!" Queen Bee yelled in anger as her flowing royal robe was pinned to the wall.

"Gotcha!" Bumblebee cheered as her opponent twisted against one of the elaborate Bialya tapestries. Queen Bee struggled to free herself, but Bumblebee used a battle-ax to cut down the heavy velvet curtains that flanked the tapestry. When they fell, the weight of the curtains crushed Queen Bee to the floor. Bumblebee grabbed a cord from the wall and used it to tie up the angry queen.

"Not bad for a girl with no powers, wouldn't you say?" said Bumblebee. Satisfied that Queen Bee could not get out of her bonds, Bumblebee pressed her suit's power button and felt her blasters charge up and the superstrength flow through her armor.

"Now if you'll excuse me," she said, "there's somewhere I need to be."

CHAPTER 37

When Bumblebee flew out of Honeycomb Hall, she was in for a shock. The gardens were starting to bloom, and the sweet scent of fragrant flowers wafted through the air. Poison Ivy was using her powers to reinvigorate the flowers, and a few Supers were following her instructions for good old-fashioned watering, fertilizing, and weeding to help all the other plant life bounce back. Lightly rolling hills were blanketed with soft green grass, and the castle walls, once dark and gray, now hosted emerald vines intertwined with pink and white flowers. Majestic trees arched to create shaded canopies, and water fountains bubbled, their sound like a gentle rain.

Beast Boy ran over to Bumblebee and hugged her so tight she had trouble breathing. "Are you okay?" Worry was etched on his face. "What happened? Where's Queen Bee?"

"She's a little tied up right now," Bumblebee said. "My parents . . . ?"

"Your mother and father are safe," Beast Boy assured her. "They were found wandering the streets of Bialya, lost and more than a little confused. Wonder Woman is flying them home in her Invisible Jet this very minute."

Bumblebee let go a sigh of relief and tried to hold back her tears. They were safe! Her mom and dad were safe.

"Poison Ivy came up with a formula to counteract any lingering effects from the fake pollen," Beast Boy continued. "She's got teams of Supers out getting all the different ecosystems back on track. The bees that were affected are pollinating once again."

Bumblebee couldn't help but grin when she heard this. "And the giant killer bees?" she asked, looking around.

Beast Boy smiled back at her. "Once Batgirl had the control box, she was able to reverse the technology that made them big. It was the most awesome thing—mid-battle, when we were all fighting these giant bees, they shrank back down to size."

Beast Boy pointed to a swarm of bees hovering nearby. "The not-so-giant bees are docile now, and so is the rest of the Royal Army. That's them over there. You should say something to them."

When Bumblebee flew over, they bowed to her, the same way they had bowed to Queen Bee. "She can't boss you around anymore," Bumblebee told them. They didn't move— all stood at rigid attention.

"They think you're their new queen," Beast Boy whispered. Bumblebee blinked in surprise. "They're awaiting your orders."

Bumblebee nodded as the weight of this news sank in. "I hereby decree," she began, "that you are free, now and forever, and will never be under anyone else's command again."

With that, the bees flew three circles of gratitude around her and then disappeared into the sky.

"You did great, Beast Boy," Bumblebee said. The raindrops on the grass sparkled like diamonds as the sun shone bright.

"It's you who's amazing," he replied. "Bumblebee, I'm so glad you got your power back and were able to capture Queen Bee!"

Bumblebee hesitated, then told him, "It's odd. All this time when I thought I didn't have any power, I was wrong. It was always there, whether or not my battery pack was working."

"I'm not sure I understand," Beast Boy said, scratching his head.

"My super suit didn't give me the power. I gave power to my super suit. The power has been right here all along," Bumblebee said, pointing to her head.

"I coulda told you that," Beast Boy said, putting his hands over his chest and pretending to swoon. "You're the real deal, Bumblebee. Now let's tell Commissioner Gordon

and the authorities in this jurisdiction where they can pick up Queen Bee, and then head home. I could use a snack!"

Just as they were about to leave, they heard a familiar voice. "Bye-bye," it said sadly. "It was nice knowing the two of you."

They turned around to see Cuckoo Bee emerge from behind the rose bushes. His eyes welled with tears.

Bumblebee's heart almost broke. "Cuckoo Bee," she said, rushing up to him, "we couldn't have done all this if it weren't for you!"

"Really?" he asked, perking up. "Aw, shucks! I mean, you told me to find the Supers, and I did! I said, 'Bumblebee's friends, follow me!'"

"You know," Bumblebee said, putting her arm around him, "Honeycomb Hall is going to need someone to take care of it. You know this place pretty well, don't you?"

Cuckoo Bee nodded. "I do," he said. He paused and then lit up. "Are you gonna be my new boss? Oh, Bumblebee, I'd really, really, really like that!"

"No, not me," Bumblebee said. Her smile was bright. "I'm not going to be the boss of you. You will be your own boss. You will be in charge of Honeycomb Hall!"

It took Cuckoo Bee a while to understand, but when he did, his smile was so big that it was contagious.

"Group hug!" shouted Beast Boy, grinning back at him.

As the three embraced, Bumblebee looked around and saw her other friends, the bees, energetically buzzing from flower to flower. Her smile grew wider. When Cuckoo Bee hugged a little too hard, she looked up and saw that a rainbow had appeared where the sky had once been gray and dark.

CHAPTER 38

The sneezing had stopped. Flowers were in full bloom, and the bees were back, busy and happy. Supergirl's Aunt Martha was so ecstatic that she baked enough honey-butter cookies for everyone at Super Hero High, and Bumblebee's fan club, the Honey Bees, were once again sending jars of honey. Since Bumblebee had more than she could use, she shared them with the local schools so that when they studied bees, each student got their own jar. And Honeycomb Hall and its glorious gardens became the number one destination in Bialya, thanks to its beloved caretaker, Cuckoo Bee, who had agreed, at Poison Ivy's insistence, to be the new host of *Greenhouse Hullabaloo.*

Several Supers stood around the Andrena-Beecher house. "Here are the architectural plans," said Hawkgirl, unfurling the blueprints Ms. Andrena-Beecher had provided.

Batgirl leaned in to study them. "Got it!" she said.

The Supers huddled and then split up, each with an assignment.

Mr. and Ms. Andrena-Beecher stood by, linking arms with their daughter as they watched the house being rebuilt before their eyes.

"You've got some pretty great friends there," her mother said appreciatively.

Bumblebee nodded. This she knew was true.

"Hey, I'm thinking of entering another vacation contest," said her father.

"NO!" his wife and daughter yelled at the same time.

"Kidding," he said. "No more contests for me!" Then he got serious. "Bumblebee, your mother and I couldn't be more proud of you."

Ms. Andrena-Beecher agreed. "We weren't sure about this super-hero thing at first. But now, well, we know this is your destiny."

Bumblebee hugged them. They watched in silence as Poison Ivy rejuvenated the Bee Tree, reversing the fall and fortifying it so that it stood tall and strong again.

"We'll have your Bee Tree Lab up and running in no time!" Hawkgirl called out.

"Thanks!" Bumblebee yelled back. She turned to Batgirl, who was working on electrical wiring, and said, "Now we've got three labs we can work in—the Bat-Bunker, the corner of

Mr. Fox's lab that he said I could turn into my own personal tech space, and the Bee Tree Lab." She turned to her parents. "You won't mind if Batgirl joins me now and then when I come home?"

"Your friends are welcome here anytime," her mom said as they watched the Supers adding the finishing touches to the new and improved Andrena-Beecher house and Bee Tree Lab.

The next day at school, Parasite was munching on another honey-butter cookie and leaning on his broom at the back of the auditorium. It was time for the monthly assembly, something everyone looked forward to.

Frost had frozen Hal Jordan's Green Lantern ring hand again in a giant ball of ice, Beast Boy had turned into a snake to scare Raven, and Cheetah and Star Sapphire were whispering, but when Principal Waller stepped onstage, everyone snapped to attention.

"I'll get right to it," she said. "The Super Hero of the Month award goes to someone who has proven themselves far and beyond what we expect from a super hero. When she first came to this school, she worried she'd never be good enough to stand among our ranks. Well, I am here to tell you that this Super is one for you to watch and learn from. Whether using her powers or just being brave in the face of overwhelming odds, she is the definition of a true super hero. This girl is the real thing.

"Bumblebee, please join me onstage!"

EPILOGUE

Later, at Capes & Cowls Café, Bumblebee and her friends were celebrating with the triple honey cake that Steve Trevor had baked for the occasion. Harley was videoing the fun, and Poison Ivy was happily talking about what she was going to do with her free time now that Cuckoo Bee was taking over her show, when Bumblebee pulled Beast Boy aside.

"My parents gave me this when I first started at Super Hero High," she said, holding out the ICE jar of honey. "Well, we didn't have it during the battle, but I think it's appropriate that we share it now. They told me it was for emergencies or special times."

"Whoa, wow!" Beast Boy exclaimed. "You'd share that with me? This is totally awesome." He paused, then added, "So are you, but if you tell anyone I said that, I'll deny it!"

"Beast Boy, I have something to ask you," Bumblebee said, sounding a tad nervous.

"What?" he asked. Beast Boy poured so much honey over

his cake that it dripped onto the floor.

"Well, Beastie," Bumblebee joked, "we've been through so much together and had so much fun—and fear!—I was wondering if you'd want to be besties." When he kept chewing, she explained. "You know, be best friends?"

Beast Boy didn't answer, but instead looked confused.

Bumblebee felt her heart sink. She was so embarrassed. Why would he want to be her best friend? Everyone knew that despite his antics, Beast Boy could be something of a loner at times.

"Never mind," Bumblebee said, trying to sound lighthearted. "It was just a weird thought."

"It sure was!" Beast Boy agreed. "Totally weird, 'cause I thought we *already were* best friends!"

While the two laughed, Poison Ivy was strolling through Centennial Park, admiring the flowers and talking to them as she passed. Suddenly, a giant shadow blocked the sunlight.

Ivy gasped, then looked up and smiled. "Oh, for a moment you scared me," she said. "How are you? You look so . . . different."

Jason Woodrue gave her a wry smile. "Do I?" he asked. He was still dressed in his tweed three-piece suit and jaunty hat. However, things were growing on him—vines, leaf sprouts, and mosses. He now looked half man, half plant.

"What a coincidence, bumping into you here," he said smugly. "Poison Ivy, I just wanted to let you know that I never liked working for you."

"Oh, I'm sorry to hear that," she said, looking shocked and dismayed.

"I'm not sorry in the least," Jason Woodrue said as a network of vines slithered up her legs and arms. Pulling out a small spray bottle, he misted her face with a dose of Queen Bee's fake pollen while she struggled. "Poison Ivy, you are now going to work for *me!*"

To be continued . . .

After writing jingles, restaurant menus, and TV shows, Lisa Yee won the prestigious Sid Fleischman Humor Award for her debut novel, *Millicent Min, Girl Genius*. Her other novels for young readers include *Stanford Wong Flunks Big-Time, Bobby vs. Girls (Accidentally)*, and several books for American Girl, plus *Warp Speed*, about a Star Trek geek. Her most recent YA novel is *The Kidney Hypothetical*. She has also written for *Huffington Post* and is a contributor to NPR.

Lisa's books have been named a Washington Post Book of the Week, a *USA Today Critics' Pick*, an NPR Best Summer Read, and more. Writing the DC Super Hero Girls series is a dream come true, says Lisa. "I get to hang out with Wonder Woman, Batgirl, Katana, and the rest of the super heroes!"

You can visit Lisa Yee at LisaYee.com.

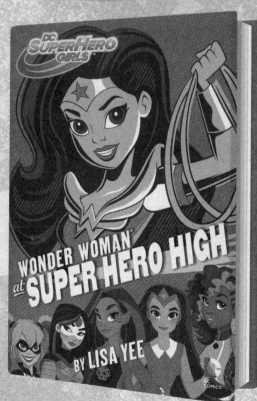

DC SuperHero Girls ™

THE TECH WIZ

SUPERPOWERS AND GEAR

- Computer Genius
- Photographic Memory
- Legendary Detective Skills
- Utility Belt
- The Latest Tech Gadget

BATGIRL at SUPER HERO HIGH

BY LISA YEE

DCSuperHeroGirls.com

DC SuperHero Girls™

THE CLASS CLOWN

SUPERPOWERS AND GEAR

- Expert Gymnast
- Acrobat
- Quick-Witted
- Mallet

DC SUPERHERO GIRLS

HARLEY QUINN at SUPER HERO HIGH

BY LISA YEE